Winning Rider

Illustrated by John Lobban

Rachel Rastrick spends every spare moment at the racing stable. She is specially involved with Catch Boy, the five-year-old hurdler. How can she prove to his trainer, regular rider, and stable lass, that he is very much more than the non-trier they think he is? How can she prove anything when her mother is determined to make her into a fashion model? But Rachel will not give in. . . .

MICHAEL HARDCASTLE

Winning Rider

A Magnet Book

Also by Michael Hardcastle
in Magnet Books

In the Net
United!
Away from Home
Free Kick
Soccer Special
Half a Team
The Saturday Horse
The Switch Horse
Fast from the Gate
Caught Out
Roar to Victory
The Team that Wouldn't Give In
Tiger of the Track

First published in 1985
by Methuen Children's Books Ltd
This Magnet edition first published 1987
by Methuen Children's Books Ltd
11 New Fetter Lane, London EC4P 4EE
Text copyright © 1985 Michael Hardcastle
Illustrations copyright © 1985 John Lobban
Cover illustration copyright © 1985 Methuen Children's Books
Printed in Great Britain by
Richard Clay Ltd, Bungay, Suffolk

ISBN 0 416 04532 4

One

Catch Boy, a five-year-old bay horse, clattered into the training hurdle, stumbled on landing and very nearly fell. Rachel, watching anxiously from the bushes at the side of the gallops, crossed as many fingers as she could manage.

'Don't make another mistake, Boy – *don't!*' she prayed under her breath.

The jockey, Bryn McWilliam, was taking no chances. With his whip in his left hand he hit the horse twice, hard, down the neck. Catch Boy's tail swished furiously but the horse didn't swerve. Rachel closed her eyes in disgust and dismay. She couldn't bear to see any thoroughbred, any horse, being mal-treated; and she had no doubt at all that Bryn was hitting Catch Boy out of spite. In Rachel's opinion, no professional jockey ever needed to strike a horse simply to make it run well. There were other means of persuasion and those were the ones that a true horseman would use.

Catch Boy approached the next hurdle. Bryn had

him settled again and there appeared to be no need for any slap to make the horse jump properly. But Bryn couldn't resist cuffing the bay lightly as he was about to take off. This time, Catch Boy twisted in mid-air. Yet, astonishingly, he landed perfectly and was immediately into his stride again. There was no sign or sound of approval from the rider, however; or, at least, none that Rachel could detect. Would Catch Boy never do anything right for Bryn McWilliam? she wondered.

'Better that time, wasn't it?' said a voice in her ear.

Rachel was thoroughly startled. She hadn't been aware of anyone's approach but Kevin Huzzard was now standing beside her, looking as worried as ever. The trainer of Catch Boy and a score of other hurdlers and steeplechasers, Mr Huzzard had once been described in a sporting newspaper as 'harrassed-looking' and Rachel thought that was an accurate description of him much of the time. Often he seemed to be thinking of several things at the same time while doing something entirely different.

'Er, yes, much better,' Rachel replied, without being quite sure what she was agreeing with; on balance, though, she supposed Mr Huzzard was referring to Catch Boy's second jump.

'Bryn doesn't think he's genuine, you know, and I'm inclined to agree with him,' Huzzard went on in a low voice. 'That must account for his poor form on the racecourse. Plenty of horses like that, you know. Show a lot of promise the first time they run and after

6

that they just sort of pack up – won't try for the life of 'em!'

'Oh, Catch Boy's not like that, Mr Huzzard!' Rachel exclaimed. 'I *know* he's not. He puts *everything* into his work when I ride him. You know he does.'

The trainer didn't appear convinced but for a few moments he simply watched the gallop in silence. By now Bryn had slowed the horse down preparatory to turning and cantering back to the watchers. Catch Boy wasn't blowing at all. He looked as fresh as if he'd just emerged from his box.

Rachel turned to glance at Kevin Huzzard, who was tall and thin as a whip. Before setting up as a trainer, a few years earlier, he had been a jockey himself, though not a particularly successful one. As he himself often remarked, he really wasn't 'the right shape for that job'. But at least it had taught him a great deal about race riding and what a jockey should be doing at various stages of a race.

It was Rachel's dearest ambition to ride against professional jockeys. In recent years girls and women had been allowed to compete on equal, or almost equal, terms with men in horse-racing. There were more girls than ever before working in stables so that the term 'stable lad' often meant 'stable lass'. The great hope of many of those girls was that they would be given sufficient chances by their boss, the trainer, to prove they had the ability to become professional jockeys. Some, however, came up against a solid barrier of prejudice in the form of male trainers who would never accept, as long as they lived, that girls could ride as successfully, and as strongly, as boys. Rachel knew she was lucky in finding someone like Mr Huzzard to work for in the evenings, at weekends and during school holidays. He always said he judged solely on the basis of ability, not sex.

Now, however, he seemed totally indifferent to her hopes. Her mention of what Catch Boy could do when she was riding brought no response from him at all for several moments. Then he spared her no more than a quick glance as he remarked:

'But you don't ride him in races, do you, girl? And racing, not larking about on the gallops, is what I'm talking about. We've got to get that horse to take life seriously and put his best efforts into earning his corn.'

Then, cuttingly, he added: 'If he has the ability to do it, that is.'

Rachel wanted to rush to the defence of her favourite racehorse but sensed it was time to be cautious. Mr Huzzard was clearly not in the best of moods that morning. No doubt he was tired, as usual, but perhaps it was more than that. He always had too much to do because, he claimed, he couldn't afford to pay extra staff. So, from before dawn until late at night, he was busy: checking on the horses, dealing with owners (who were forever ringing him up to inquire about the health and form of their horses), buying provisions for stable and staff and himself, coping with vets and farriers and salesmen, driving the horse-box to and from either the races or horse sales – and, on top of all that, attending to the business of being a trainer by seeing that the horses were entered for appropriate races in the weeks ahead. That, as Rachel knew from the times she'd assisted him on Sunday evenings, was just about the most time-consuming job of all. If he made a mistake in entering or withdrawing a horse from a particular race he wouldn't just lose a chance of success, and therefore a winning bonus for himself and the stable: he could easily lose the confidence of an owner, who would then take his horses away to put them with another and, so the owner would claim, more efficient trainer. That was Kevin Huzzard's chief nightmare, she knew, so she couldn't help wondering whether, that morning, he'd received a phone call from a dissatisfied or irate owner.

'Well, what do you think?' he asked Bryn McWilliam as the jockey reined in his mount in front of him. 'Is this one turning into a real dog?'

Rachel, from her experience of working in the stable for almost a year, knew what that term meant: that the horse was a non-trier, mulish and unresponsive to normal training methods.

Much to her surprise, Bryn gave her a quick, sidelong glance before he replied. 'He's a bit *difficult* at present – not sure what's got into him,' was the verdict.

Rachel was surprised again. She'd expected him to

commit himself completely. Bryn wasn't usually half-hearted in his opinions. Still, she was thankful that Catch Boy hadn't been condemned outright. That could have been the beginning of the end of Catch Boy's career in the care of Kevin Huzzard, Master of Mintonbury Magna (the official name of his training stables and an inflated one for what was really a rather run-down establishment, much in need of new woodwork and fresh paint). Horses which didn't earn their keep on the track were simply a drain on the resources of owner and trainer.

Kevin Huzzard nodded as if Bryn's words were exactly what he'd expected to hear.

'Right, well, we'll just have to see what we can do to sort him out,' he said resignedly. 'Maybe Rachel here can think of something that'll work. The female mind is supposed to be unpredictable, so we can all keep our fingers crossed, eh?'

Rachel assumed he was being humorous and so she smiled and said cheerfully: 'I'll do my best, Mr Huzzard. I honestly think he's a pretty good horse.'

She would have said more but she was aware of Bryn's brooding brown eyes: he was watching her and she didn't want to antagonise him completely. After all, she had to spend a fair amount of time in his company at the stables. She knew that if he found opportunities to complain to the trainer about her work or attitude, Mr Huzzard might easily decide to do without her services. He wouldn't want friction between the people looking after his thoroughbred horses, some of whom were highly-strung and very sensitive to the moods and temperament of the human beings around them.

Moreover, Bryn, although only a few years older than Rachel, was the stable-jockey. He'd ridden a number of winners, including some for other stables, and so was in a powerful position to influence the trainer's thinking and actions.

Catch Boy edged towards her, scenting the possibility of a mint, her usual titbit for him. She had a packet in her pocket but suspected that it wasn't the moment to reward the horse. Bryn, for one, certainly wouldn't approve.

'Isn't it time you got off to school?' the jockey asked suddenly.

Rachel made a show of studying her watch, although she knew perfectly well what time it was. The underlying unfairness of the question didn't surprise her at all. Bryn seemed always to want to get in a dig about her age or lack of experience.

'I suppose so,' she replied, reaching up to tweak Boy's left ear, something he either liked or disliked intensely according to his mood.

This time the horse backed away until he got a sharp slap and a sharper word from Bryn. Sometimes the lads used bad language in her presence just to see what her reaction would be. She wondered what they would say if she used even stronger language to them. As it was, Bryn's rudeness brought no rebuke this time from Mr Huzzard, who had switched his attention to another horse in his string that was proving fractious. In any case, the trainer tended to take the view that those who worked for him should learn to stand up for themselves.

'See you Friday evening,' she called to Kevin Huzzard and got a wave of his hand in acknowledgement.

The weekend was what she looked forward to from the beginning of every week. Saturdays especially were her favourite time. On that day the trainer and many of his staff were away at the races and so she had the stables almost to herself in the afternoons. If Catch Boy wasn't racing then she could devote much of her time to him. She never tired of being with him

and he seemed to enjoy her company in his box. Most horses, she had been told, disliked solitude and became increasingly resentful if left on their own for long periods.

She retrieved her bike from the bushes. As she pedalled away from the training-gallops she reflected, not for the first time, how much happier she'd be if she were riding a horse instead of an old push bike. One day, though, her school life would be over and she could spend all her days with horses. Meanwhile, she needed to move a little faster if she was to avoid trouble by being late for registration at the Comprehensive.

With a deep sigh she lowered her head and began to pedal much harder.

Two

Annajane leaned against the gatepost for support as she tried to control her mirth. Rachel had never seen her best friend so overcome with laughter. Her convulsions were so strong, it seemed to Rachel, there was a danger the gate might be loosened from its hinges. But then, Annajane was a solidly-built girl.

'Honestly, AJ, it wasn't *that* funny – it was just Guido being his usual self, full of himself and his beloved Frog tongue,' said Rachel, shaking her head in disbelief at her friend's explosive reaction to the French master's criticism of her latest attempt to speak conversational French. Guy Hill was the teacher's name but, inevitably, the pupils had immediately translated that into Guido Colline.

Annajane, however, was determined to make the most of the occasion. Now she started to quote Mr Hill again, producing a very passable imitation of his style as well as his accent.

'Oh, you terr-i-ble child, but-chering our beautiful language again, the language of the a-ris-tocracy that

14

you are rendering into the dri-vel of the gu-tter. *Oui, mam'selle, la gouttière*!' Then she became herself again. 'Oh, Guido, you *are* priceless – priceless. Oh, Rae, if only he could *hear* himself. He'd resign immediately if he had a grain of self-awareness in his body. Honestly, where *did* the school find him?'

Rachel shrugged. 'Well, I think he's a bit more interesting than that supply teacher we had last term. He was so dull I can't even remember his name. At least Guido gives you a laugh, provides you with a bit of entertainment on a grey day.'

She paused and then added: 'Anyway, you should be keen to learn all the French you can if you're going to be a fashion designer. I mean, isn't France supposed to be the top nation for fashion? The Paris fashion show gets terrific publicity.'

Annajane shrugged. 'Oh, I'll get by on the French I already know. The thing is, the French will be coming to *me* and speaking in *English* because they need the results of my brilliant talent. Another thing: you don't need French for physiotherapy. The language of the body speaks for itself – hey, that's a good line, isn't it? I must –'

'Physiotherapy?' Rachel cut in, eyebrows raised. 'What's that got to do with anything you were talking about?'

'Oh, didn't I tell you?' Annajane asked innocently.

'Tell me what? Oh, come on, AJ, you really can be infuriating sometimes. I haven't got all night to hang around the school gates and talk nonsense with you.

I've got to –'

'– go and muck out some horses, I know. But listen: I *must* have mentioned that I have decided to combine my design work with physiotherapy. It'll work together like a charm! I'll tell all my customers just what to wear in future while I pummel 'em into shape for the clothes I've designed. Smart, don't you think? Getting two old birds with one shot.'

'But you said you wanted to create clothes for the young. Well, they won't want physiotherapy as well. You'll only get old folk who want your kind of fashion.'

'Wrong, Rae, wrong, wrong, wrong! You seem to forget that we haven't all got neat little figures like yours – almost the little boy look. Lots of girls find it pretty impossible to get rid of extra, unwanted flesh – well, they find it impossible to do it by themselves, anyway. I should know, mate! I have to work like stink to keep my weight down, you know that, Rae.'

Rachel didn't answer. She was thinking about Annajane's comment on her figure. In fact, although she was grateful for the slimness of her build – for one thing, it ensured that she, unlike many jockeys, wouldn't have weight problems – she was aware that it didn't provide all the strength she needed for riding. She could have done with some of Annajane's muscles but she didn't want to say that. Although she might from time to time joke about it, her friend was really very self-conscious about her own figure.

Easing herself away from the school's perimeter

wall, Rachel led the way towards the town centre. She had things to think about and would have preferred to be on her own. Sometimes, Annajane's company was either tedious or juvenile, or both; but Rachel needed someone to talk to, someone to confide in, from time to time, and Annajane Wentworth had many good qualities. For a start, she was loyal to her friends, and loyalty was important – as important perhaps as anything. Annajane could certainly be relied upon to take Rachel's side whenever there was a risk of parental interference in her plans. Annajane herself suffered only rarely from the disapproval of her parents. They seemed not to care too much what she got up to outside – or even inside – the home.

Rachel, on the other hand, was constantly having to win over her mother before she could pursue her ambition to ride racehorses. Mrs Rastrick was quite definite in her views about what Rachel should be doing with her life; and they didn't include support for working in a stable. Annajane was also sympathetic to Rachel's interest in horses, though she herself, as she bluntly put it, 'couldn't care less about dumb animals'. She did concede, however, that of all the dumb animals in existence the horse was the most beautiful or, rather, as Rachel insisted, the *thoroughbred* horse.

When she was younger Rachel had petted ponies and jumped at gymkhanas and stuck up rows of rosettes on her bedroom walls. But it was a racehorse that she fell in love with, a black horse of stunning beauty with elegance in every step it took. It was, she discovered, trained by Kevin Huzzard and it was from him that she learned her first lesson about race-horses: never describe one as 'black' because in racing that's unlucky; instead, call it 'brown' even though its coat contains hardly a speck of that colour. She'd vowed then that one day she would win a race on a brown horse; and when she was rich enough from her riding fees and prize money she would own such a horse. Since then, the character of the horse had come to mean as much to her as its colour. Nowadays everything had to be measured in her estimation against the special qualities possessed by Catch Boy.

'You thinking about that dumb racehorse of yours?' Annajane inquired as they reached a road junction. The physiotherapist-to-be didn't enjoy lengthy silences at any time.

'What else is there *worth* thinking about?' Rachel responded airily. She didn't expect to be taken seriously but Annajane was plainly a bit miffed.

'Well, I was hoping you were thinking about what I've just told you – you know, about physiotherapy. I'd've been interested in your opinion, actually, sur-prise, surprise. But obviously you couldn't care less.'

'Sorry, AJ, truly. I didn't mean to be rude. Point is, I really am trying to sort out what to do about Catch Boy. I mean, how can I persuade the trainer that Bryn is riding him all wrong? Oh, and get him – the trainer I mean – to give me a go on the horse in a

18

real race? But forget it, AJ, forget it. It's my problem and I'll solve it.

'So, yes, I am thinking about your new craze – *sorry* – I do take it seriously. In fact, it seems quite a clever arrangement. Just so long as you don't want to use me as a guinea-pig to work your theories out on. I need to build muscle-power and physio's not designed for that, is it?'

'Well, I should be able to come up with something that would help. Tell you what, I'll get my textbooks out and see what they recommend. But it'll be good for one thing for you, Rae – I'll know how to deal with all your bruises and sprains after you fall off a horse!'

'Oh, great, thanks very much! I have complete faith in you, too!'

'No, come off it, Rae, every rider falls off some time. Bound to. Part of the game, I thought. So then you need a physio to attend to you and get you back in top shape. In fact, you can do me a real favour when I get started because you'll know lots of jockeys and they'll all need my services as a top physio. You can recommend me and then I might even solve your own little problems for free. That's fair, isn't it?'

Rachel nodded, anxious now to get home, hurry through a meal and be at the stables in time to see the horses before they were settled down for the night. 'Evening stables' was the official name for the trainer's tour of inspection, looking into each box, with the lad or lass present, to check that the inmate was in good health and as comfortable as could be for the night. There were often little jobs that needed doing once the paid staff went off duty and Rachel liked to make herself available for them. After all, Kevin Huzzard was the one person who could get her into racing as a rider: thus if she was helpful to him, he would surely do his best for her. Her father had once remarked, while reading a newspaper story about a government appointment, that it wasn't *what* you knew but *who* you knew that enabled you to get on in life. Rachel believed him.

They parted outside a chemist's shop where Annajane wanted to inspect the stock to see what was new in the field of potions and lotions: she was a firm believer in good planning and so was already thinking about what would be good for the health of her future clients.

'*Au revoir – à demain,*' she said in the most atrocious, exaggerated accent as she parted from her friend. Then she laughed. She was back in her old form.

'Yeah, see you tomorrow – unless I'm required at short notice to ride a champion horse at Cheltenham!'

That, as Annajane well knew, was Rachel's greatest desire: and to achieve it she would make almost any sacrifice in life.

As soon as she got home Rachel sensed that her mother was dying to impart some special news. Rachel's heart sank. It couldn't, she was certain, be good news for her so, deliberately, she didn't give her mother an opening. The longer the announcement was delayed the better, in Rachel's opinion. If, as she supposed, her mother had plans for her then there was no point in adding to the time she'd have to spend fighting them.

'Had a good day, darling?' Mrs Rastrick asked brightly as she prepared some tea.

'So-so,' was the familiar non-committal reply.

Of course, there was no mention of the early morning visit to the training-gallops. Mrs Rastrick had been watching from the kitchen window when her daughter returned on her bike before setting off to school on foot. There had been no mention of it then, either, though Rachel had seen the usual disapproval on her mother's lips. The subject of Rachel's involvement with horses was ignored at all times unless it was absolutely impossible to avoid referring to it.

They had started their meal, which featured a very uninspired fish pie, when Mrs Rastrick realised she could contain her news no longer. Rachel, who was absorbed by her thoughts of Catch Boy, at first didn't grasp what her mother was talking about. When she did, she slammed down her knife and fork with a force that threatened to crack the plate.

'Mother, I'm not going anywhere on a Saturday afternoon, not for any reason in the world! You know my Saturdays are – are sacred!'

'Don't use that word, Rachel, not about *horse-racing*. There's nothing sacred about racing silly horses. I've gone to a lot of trouble to arrange this

appointment for you. I'm only sorry it couldn't be this coming Saturday. Still, Saturday week's not far away.'

'I won't go!' Rachel muttered between clenched teeth.

She felt sick to the pit of her stomach, and the quality of the fish pie was not the cause. Her mother would enlist the support of her husband, there was no doubt about that; Colin Rastrick always took the easy way out. He didn't like arguments and so he nearly always sided with his wife. Therefore he would order Rachel to attend the model agency photographic session the following week. Rachel couldn't see any way in which she could get out of it.

'Look,' her mother was saying in what she regarded as a soft, reasonable tone, 'this could be a real breakthrough for you, darling. It could be the making of any young girl with good looks and a good figure. A chance to be seen by top fashion photographers – well, the top people in fashion, anyway. Why, you could be modelling really beautiful clothes in no time at all. You could easily fit in future sessions in the evenings and at weekends. Most girls of your age would give their right arm for a chance like this!'

'If they had an arm amputated *no* photographer would want them. Talk sense,' Rachel replied scathingly. She no longer cared what her mother would say about rudeness or what threats she'd make about restricting Rachel's freedom.

'That sort of remark is just not worthy of you, Rachel. It's not worthy of any *intelligent* girl,' her mother said severely.

'If I'm intelligent then I shouldn't be expected to model clothes – that's a job for a *dummy*,' was the retaliatory answer. 'Intelligence is wasted if all you do is hang frilly clothes on it.'

Predictably, Mrs Rastrick gave out a large and heavy sigh. Rachel knew just what her mother was going to say: and Mrs Rastrick said it.

'There's nothing intelligent about sitting on a horse, my girl. *Anybody* can do it. All it means is that you get a fat bottom and fat thighs and generally just look horsey and not a bit attractive. It might be different if you were a man, Rachel. I know there are good careers for the likes of Lester Piggott and that little Willie Carson and those sort of people. For a girl like you there's nothing of that kind, nothing at all.'

Rachel remained tight-lipped, letting her mother rumble on in familiar fashion.

'Now, to have the opportunity to wear all those pretty, those *luxurious* clothes, is a delight. And to be paid really good money for it into the bargain, well, I can't imagine any normal girl refusing the chance. I've told you umpteen times, to get on in this life you've got to plan ahead. So now's the time to be making positive arrangements about your future. School doesn't last for ever, you know.'

Calmly now, Rachel was studying her mother. In spite of strenuous attempts to keep her weight in check Mrs Rastrick was looking, to Rachel's eyes, distinctly chubby. She didn't really help her own cause, either, by regularly wearing trousers which merely emphasised her expanding girth. She had light blue eyes and a round face and quite beautiful hands. Her husband was thin and tall with chocolate brown eyes. Spouses, Rachel had read, were supposed to resemble each other, either from the start or later on in their partnership. Well, that certainly could not be said of Mr and Mrs Rastrick.

What baffled Rachel was that she herself took after neither of her parents; and that, according to the experience of her friends, was definitely unusual.

More than once it had crossed her mind that she wasn't their child at all. Surely it was normal for the offspring to resemble one parent or the other in physical terms or, at the very least, to share some of their characteristics: a gesture or a way of holding oneself, a hint within a smile or just a similarity in walking. So, either a mistake had been made at the hospital where she was born, or she had been adopted. After all, they hadn't had another child, had they? If there was a dark secret in her parents' lives then it was natural they'd want to keep it from her until she was old enough (in their opinion, that is) to be able to cope with it. It might explain why her mother was so anxious to plan her life for her. She wouldn't want Rachel to make the same mistake as she had made – whatever that mistake was.

'Did you hear what I said?' Mrs Rastrick was asking.

Rachel supposed she had heard, though already she couldn't remember what had really been said. Her mind was still on the subject of her origins. Occasionally she'd tried to discover the truth by asking a devious question that just might, by its apparent innocence, have provoked a revealing reply. So far, no luck. But one of these days, she vowed, she would really challenge her parents: ask them outright whose daughter she was. That would probably cause an explosion with an effect like a volcano erupting. But they deserved to be shaken: they'd hurt her often enough by their total lack of understanding.

'Yes, I heard,' she said, and then promptly filled her mouth with fish and potatoes and grilled cheese.

'Well, then, I want you to understand this, Rachel,' her mother went on relentlessly. 'If you don't keep that appointment at the model agency, AND do your level best to impress them – if you don't then I can promise you this, young lady: you'll never set foot again in that stable yard you're so attached to. Your father and I will see to that. Do you understand?'

'Yes, mother,' said Rachel, swallowing the last portion of the humble pie.

That was what she said. But she was thinking that a lot could happen before Saturday week arrived.

Three

Rachel flexed her fingers in an effort to counteract the tingling in her wrists and forearms. Her routine exercises with the dumb-bells to strengthen her arms had been as vigorous as usual. She always felt that if she ached afterwards then they must have been doing her good. They were also her way of warming up after getting out of bed on a chill autumn morning before there was any hope of much daylight.

Before starting on her squatting-and-jumping-high exercise, a particularly energetic routine favoured by the army and designed to strengthen thigh muscles, she took a peep between the curtains of her bedroom window. Not a light to be seen anywhere: except, oh yes, one had just been switched on at the end house on the other side of the park. That, as she well knew, was the home of old Mr Thornton. He had once worked with horses and liked talking about those days whenever he could ambush Rachel. Usually, she didn't mind because he sometimes passed on useful snippets of information about how to get the best out of some types of horses. Saturday was the day he always got up early so that he could study the newspapers for the form of the horses he intended to back. It was a theory of his that most horses were sent out to win on Saturdays: for one thing, the prize money was better than on weekdays, and for another, trainers and jockeys enjoyed being seen on television. According to Mr Thornton, on weekdays there were too many horses not trying to win because jockeys and trainers were holding them back for richer pickings.

Rachel thought he exaggerated a lot but perhaps there was some truth in what he said. She knew hardly anything about that side of racing, the dishonest side as she thought of it. Some of the girls from other stables whispered about horses being 'stopped' by various tricks, including being given a bucket of water just before racing, but Rachel dismissed those sort of stories as useful excuses for horses that didn't win. So far as she could tell, Kevin Huzzard sent his horses out with the intention of winning every race they could. On the other hand, it had to be admitted that they didn't win very often. Today, though, it might be different because Catch Boy was running at Chesterfield in a two-mile hurdle for novices. If he won that race then surely he would become practically the star of the stable instead of being a candidate for the sale ring.

As she strenuously continued with her muscles-building routine Rachel reviewed the bay's prospects. She needed to think of something pleasant to counteract the agony of the exercises. Unfortunately, she couldn't really hold out much hope for Catch Boy, particularly as Bryn would be riding him. The horse would be aware that his jockey had no faith in him and so would almost certainly race accordingly. And Bryn, determined to increase his tally of winners, would belabour the horse as much as the laws of racing would allow. Catch Boy would return to the unsaddling enclosure with weals on his flanks where he'd been struck with the whip.

One of the few things which she disliked about horse-racing was the use of the whip, even by the most skilful and successful riders. What's more, most owners and trainers seemed to feel that hitting a horse was essential in many cases if it was to have any chance of winning. Trouble was, as she had not yet taken part in a flying finish where each jockey had to get the best out of his mount, she couldn't argue with such experts that whips weren't necessary – ever!

One day, though, she intended to prove it – by riding a winner in the tightest of finishes by using just hands and heels. That would show 'em!

The torso-torture over for the day, she hurriedly dressed in old but warm clothes and put away the dumb-bells. Her parents, she hoped, were still asleep and wouldn't wake before she left the house. Although they didn't any longer attempt to prevent her Saturday visits to the stables, they were inclined to make disparaging remarks. Most mornings Rachel contented herself with cereal and a hot drink, usually a meat extract. On racing days, as she thought of them, she needed something more substantial: work in the yard involved a lot of physical effort, from humping bales of hay to pushing a horse around his box so that she could groom him properly. So by the time the stable lads and lasses had their break, after mucking out and taking their charges on to the gallops, everyone was ready for a feed. Rachel, however, felt she wasn't always welcome round the big dining-room table with the other workers; sometimes she detected signs of resentment, as if they feared that one day she would be taking the job of one of them. So she didn't like to appear to be too eager to share their food. It was far better to eat before she got to the stables and then simply have a snack with them at break-time.

Now she whipped up some scrambled eggs re-inforced by grated cheese and wholemeal toast. That would sustain her for the rest of the morning whatever she was called upon to do.

Mr Thornton attempted to detain her as she cycled past his house. Inevitably, he'd noted that Kevin Huzzard had a couple of runners at Chesterfield and he wanted to know if she had any 'inside information,' as he put it. Rachel thought it was an excuse to chat because he obviously did like her.

'Sorry, Mr Thornton, but I can't give you much hope of a win with either Catch Boy or Hipperholme,' she told him as he leaned over his gate, listening

intently. 'I know Mr Huzzard is disappointed with both of them. Hipperholme is probably still not over the virus he had in the summer. He completely ran out of steam in his first race and Bryn McWilliam thinks he needs more time to be back at his best. Oh, and they think he has far too much weight, too.'

'Well, that's all worth knowing, young Rachel, but it's not helping me to find my winners, is it? Chesterfield's on the telly this afternoon and I really fancied the chance of cheering home a local winner – with my little bet on it, of course.'

'But maybe I've helped you by putting you off a couple of *losers*,' she pointed out, twirling the pedals of her cycle to indicate she was in a hurry and ought to be on her way without further delay.

'Do you think you'll be going to Chesterfield?' he persisted. 'If you do, love, I hope you'll give a little wave when you know the camera's on you. I'll take it that's just for me, if you do. Why I –'

'Oh, there's no chance of that, Mr Thornton! My job is to help take care of the horses which *aren't* at the races. Look, I'll be terribly late if I don't push on. 'Bye then. Hope you pick some winners.'

She'd been wondering if she'd get a chance to see a television set herself during the afternoon. Now that Catch Boy would be at the races she'd have more time to do other things. She hoped to catch a glimpse of her favourite horse both in the paddock and during the race. Quite often, though, so many races were televised during the afternoon that there wasn't time for lingering looks at the preliminary proceedings in the paddock; all you saw were details of the betting while the horses were lining up for the start; and then, the race itself. If your horse wasn't in the leading bunch and made no significant forward move during the race then you might never see it at all. Naturally enough, the cameras tracked the leaders and tended to ignore the also-rans. Rachel, though, had her fingers crossed that one of these days she'd have the unalloyed pleasure of watching Catch Boy cruise to the front after the last hurdle and win, as trainers sometimes said, by the length of a street. After that, the cameras would concentrate on him as he was fêted in the winners' enclosure by Richard Cayley, the owner, and the trainer; and was admired by everyone. She wasn't going to commit her thoughts about the identity of Catch Boy's jockey.

There was the usual air of controlled frenzy about the activities in the yard when she free-wheeled into the stables at Mintonbury Magna. Nobody was permitted to yell or make loud noises in case they upset the horses. Even curses had to be uttered under the breath. All the same, it was impossible to disguise the anxiety to get jobs done in time, especially on a racing-day when so much had to be crammed into too little time. Instinctively, Rachel glanced across at Catch Boy's box; the top half of the door was open but there was no sign of the horse, which, she guessed, meant that someone was already attending to him. She hoped it wasn't Bryn.

After parking her bike behind the tack room she was making her way to Catch Boy's box when Kevin Huzzard suddenly emerged from the back door of his house, which adjoined the stable yard.

'Ah, Rachel, there you are,' he said, frowning, as if to show that he'd been waiting for her to turn up and wasn't pleased she hadn't arrived earlier. 'Got a job for you.'

Her heart plummeted. That surely meant something pretty unpleasant, like having to muck out several more horses; or it could even mean that she was being asked to look after another horse instead of Catch Boy. Whatever it was, she was in no position to refuse if she was to remain in favour with the trainer.

'Yes, Mr Huzzard?' she said as cheerfully as she

could manage.

'Do you think you could manage to take charge of Catch Boy at Chesterfield?' he asked to her total amazement. 'Nicola has gone down with that dratted virus, *she* says. Damned nuisance. I'm short-handed as it is. But if you could take over her duties that'd be a weight off my mind. Probably give you a couple of quid for your pains if you cope all right. What about it?'

Rachel couldn't imagine a more thrilling offer; she guessed he knew that. But it was always Mr Huzzard's way to treat most things in a matter-of-fact fashion, displaying no noticeable pleasure in someone else's excitement.

'That's just terrific, Mr Huzzard. Honestly, you know I'll do whatever is wanted.'

'Good, good,' he said, and this time clearly meant it. But already he was moving off, hurrying away to the next job, the next instruction to be given. 'We'll be leaving about 11 o'clock so make sure the horse is absolutely ready by then. And yourself, of course. Allen will fill you in on anything else you need to know.'

Allen Smith was Head Lad and Rachel usually got on with him quite well, though he didn't often say much. As Nicola once put it, Allen led by example, not by voice. But he could get very cross indeed if anyone made what he regarded as a stupid mistake, one that could have been avoided by just a little thought.

34

Catch Boy put his head over the door the moment he heard her step. He looked as bright, as welcoming as ever. Whenever she saw him her heart gave a jump of sheer physical pleasure, rather like a happy hiccup.

'Hey,' she said softly, reaching up to scratch under his neck with one hand and unbolt the door with the other, 'you're looking *terrific*, do you know that, Boy? You look good enough to win the Champion Hurdle in record time.'

He knew that she had an apple in her pocket and he tried to persuade her to hand it over at once. But that wasn't part of the agreement. He couldn't have it until after breakfast and before that he had to go off with the rest of the string for a pipe-opening canter. On a day when he was racing he wouldn't be asked to do any serious work on the gallops. A smooth canter with possibly a final sprint was all that he needed.

She checked his hay-net and saw he'd polished off the contents during the night. Saturday was a special feeding day, whether the horse raced or not, because in the evening all of them had a mixture of linseed and barley mash, eaten warm and most evidently relished by all of them. Allen Smith had a ritual on Saturdays of soaking the linseed and barley overnight and then cooking it until midday. He tended to treat his charges like a devoted chef. Food, he always said, was the fuel that powered a horse home to the winning-post, so it had to be of the best.

Mucking-out was not Rachel's favourite occupation (but then she didn't know anybody who enjoyed that job) but she was used to it. With Catch Boy now tied up, she wielded her pitchfork swiftly and efficiently, flicking unsoiled straw into a heap on one side; and placing the rest, along with the droppings, on to a muck-sack by the door. When the sack was full, she gathered the corners together, heaved and twisted in practically the same movement, swung it over her shoulder and trudged off to dispose of the contents.

She arrived at the big heap at the same time as Cheryl, one of the newest members of the staff. As Rachel had discovered from conversations with and about her, Cheryl was thoroughly ambitious and determined to succeed as a rider. Rachel would have been happy to make friends with her but it was clear that Cheryl regarded her as something of a rival.

'Some people seem to have all the luck, or just know how to get what they want,' Cheryl remarked to her.

'Sorry?' said Rachel, having no idea what the other girl meant.

'You know what I mean, getting yourself to the races in charge of a runner when you aren't even employed here, just a casual who drops in when she feels like it.'

Cheryl was a muscular girl with surprisingly long fingers. She wasn't at all careless but as she tipped her sack on to the heap, she somehow managed to spill some of the contents over Rachel's jeans and boots. She didn't apologise.

Rachel decided it was best to ignore such spite, for

she was sure that's what it was. 'Look, I "do" Catch Boy whenever Nicola's having time off, or whatever,' she pointed out reasonably, 'so it's only fair I should get the chance to go racing with him when she's not here. It's not my fault, Cheryl, that Nicola's got a bug or something.'

'It's not my fault, either, that I get landed with a couple of crocks like Packed Lunch and Scalpel. God knows when either of them will be fit enough to do a proper gallop let alone run a decent race. The guv'nor knows that so he ought to let me have a bit of an outing when the chance comes up, like today at Chesterfield. But no, *you* get to go. And you're just *playing* at being a stable lass!'

'No, I'm not!' Rachel protested hotly. 'Just as soon as I get away from school I'm coming here to work full time. Mr Huzzard has promised me that. I'm not taking anybody's job today, you know that. I'm just filling in.'

'And one of these days you just might *get* filled in,' Cheryl muttered darkly, turning away to return to her two invalids.

Rachel sympathised with Cheryl even though she couldn't bring herself to like her. It was true about her two horses. Packed Lunch was, by general agreement, a bit of a nutter. To get him to work at all he had to be taken to the gallops by a different route each day. He had to be kidded that life was full of surprises, all for his benefit. Then, just when it appeared he was on the verge of full fitness again, he would

38

develop heat in a leg or cut into himself by over-reaching (when a hind hoof cut into a foreleg), so he would be on the 'easy' list again for a few days until it was thought he could stand another dose of training. In those circumstances it wasn't surprising that Cheryl felt frustrated.

Scalpel didn't help her cause for he, too, was an invalid. He'd been pin-fired – an operation to strengthen a leg – and wouldn't be ready to return to active duty for several more weeks at the very earliest. But that was the luck of the draw because newcomers to a stable had to take what was available and it was hardly likely their horses would be the star performers. Rachel thought it was ironic that a horse with a name like Scalpel should be on the sick list following a surgical operation. Of course Cheryl wasn't likely to see a joke in that.

When, a little later, the first string wended their way on to the gallops Rachel found that Cheryl wasn't the only person to speak sharply to her that morning.

She was riding Catch Boy only because Bryn McWilliam was in the saddle on Hipperholme, the stable's other runner at Chesterfield. Normally the jockey would have exercised both horses on the morning of a race but the guv'nor wanted Bryn to pop another novice chaser over a couple of training fences in readiness for an outing on Monday.

As Catch Boy broke into a canter Bryn ranged alongside her.

'Don't overdo it on this fella,' he shouted across. 'I

want him fresh for this race today, not half-dead from being over-galloped.'

Rachel was furious. She'd already been given her instructions from the trainer and she was used to obeying him to the letter. Anyone who hoped to be a jockey knew it was madness to go against orders either on the gallops or on the racecourse. Trainers relied heavily on jockeys doing what they were told and then reporting their findings so that the trainer could properly assess the horse's fitness and progress.

She was inclined to shout a stinging retort but somehow she managed to remain calm: and silent. Let Bryn work it out for himself, she decided. He allowed her to lead him but kept station at her girths. She knew he was practically daring her to increase the pace. But Catch Boy was perfectly happy to cruise along, working well within himself. He gave Rachel the feeling that he was totally relaxed: as, indeed, he usually did when they were on the gallops together. In her experience, he was wonderfully placid and adaptable.

Even when Bryn metaphorically pressed the accelerator and Hipperholme surged ahead Catch Boy was content to keep on at his original pace. It was as if he sensed that both he and his rider were out to enjoy themselves in a very sedate way.

Some horses express their well-being with great exuberance, as Rachel had seen often enough, but Catch Boy just *flowed* as he covered the ground. It was a wonderful feeling. Whenever she was riding him on the gallops she felt she was in a world of her own where Boy himself was hers, and hers alone. It never occurred to her then that he had an owner and a trainer and Nicola, who looked after him most of the time. She and Catch Boy were *one*. She couldn't imagine a more delicious or satisfying experience; she couldn't believe anything better would happen in the rest of her life.

When they turned at the end of the stretch by the bushes Hipperholme almost veered across Catch Boy's path. Rachel knew that Bryn had performed that manoeuvre deliberately. From a distance it might be thought that she was in the wrong by not turning fast enough. Bryn had an armoury of such tricks.

'Oh, get out of the way, *Raz*,' he called. 'You ought to learn to wake that horse up!'

She hated that nickname. Jockeys often called each other by odd names; and the shorter those names were the better when they were shouted during a race ('Move over, Ben, give us some daylight!'). She had to grit her teeth to prevent herself from reacting visibly.

The trainer nodded his approval as they pulled up at the end of the gallop. His professional eye had noted each horse's stride, its breathing, the glow of its coat. Both, he decided, were ready to race. How they would perform was entirely another matter. But everyone knew how desperately anxious he was to have another winner. A winner, even of the most minor race, had a way of injecting new hope and confidence into a stable. The world seemed a brighter, more cheerful place after a winner.

There was no more unpleasantness from Cheryl when Rachel joined the rest of the lads and lasses to collect their horses' feeds from the Head Lad. People jostled good-naturedly for space in the minute feed-room until Allen pointed out that everyone would be made to wait another five minutes if they didn't behave like civilised human beings and await their turn. Each lad held out his own bowl or bowls and stated the horses' names even though, of course, Allen Smith knew them well enough. Then, after sieving the oats in a ruminative way to get rid of dust and husks, he apportioned the due amount of oats, bran, chopped hay and carrots for each of them according to their fitness and how soon they would be racing.

He gave Rachel a half-grin as Catch Boy's breakfast was poured out.

'No extra titbits from you, today, mind,' he told her. 'Mustn't over-weight him with goodies, lass.'

That was the most friendly comment she'd had so far that day and it cheered her greatly. She began to look forward to the trip to Chesterfield with genuine pleasure. She even began to imagine what it would be like if Catch Boy produced the best form of his life – and won.

Four

Kevin Huzzard had a theory that nothing ruined a horse's chances more than a bad journey to the race-course. So, although he claimed he couldn't afford even the tyres let alone the rest of the vehicle, he had recently invested in a new horse-box. It wasn't brand-new because it had been used for a short time by another trainer who'd been forced to give up racing through illness; but it was absolutely up-to-date, easy to clean and, best of all, provided a wonderfully smooth ride for horses and humans alike.

While Allen drove and chatted to Lorraine, who was not only the lass who looked after Hipperholme but was acknowledged to be Allen's girlfriend, Rachel travelled in the back with the horses. Besides being discreet it enabled her to spend more time with Catch Boy. It also gave her the opportunity to add some extra gloss to his coat and all the leather he would carry. By the time they reached Chesterfield his bridle, in particular, was practically glistening. There wasn't much doubt he appreciated her company, though she made a point of not neglecting the stable's other runner. Hipperholme was really the colour of a weatherworn stone wall and he possessed a very placid temperament. Sometimes horses that didn't get on at all together became travelling companions with the result that at least one of them finished the trip in a sweat through being so stirred up. That situation ought to have guaranteed a poor performance on the racetrack: yet it wasn't always the case. It appeared that some horses needed to get their adrenalin flowing long before they were required to race.

Rachel was thankful that she kept a change of clothing at the stables for emergencies. It meant that she, too, could look her best – or, at least, better – as she led Catch Boy round and round the parade ring. She would have hated to be seen by anyone, let alone a large crowd, in stained jeans and even grubbier anorak. Now that she had just the horses for company she could change at leisure.

She had never been to Chesterfield before but one of her hobbies was reading books about the history of racing and its famous personalities. So she knew that Chesterfield was where one of the most celebrated jockeys of all time, Fred Archer, had ridden his first winner. The track had closed down for very many years but now was popular with jumping enthusiasts. The finishing straight was particularly short and many horses had come to grief at the final obstacle because riders were determined not to be left with too much to do on the run-in to the finishing-post. They asked for an extra good jump at the fence or hurdle and sometimes the horse took off too soon or simply jumped too high. A jump should be made in a low curve, not in the form of a peak like an isosceles triangle.

As she finished dressing she noticed Catch Boy starting to nod with a rhythmic motion as if he approved of her appearance. She laughed at the thought. In fact, the five-year-old bay invariably went into his nodding routine when he was pleased with life. Rachel had once attempted to discuss Catch Boy's habits with Nicola and had been amazed to learn that Nicola had never noticed that particular trick. It had to mean either that Nicola wasn't very observant or the horse didn't do his nodding for her.

They reached the racecourse and parked dutifully in line with all the other horse-boxes from Lambourn and Newmarket and Malton and seemingly every little racing establishment in the land.

After unloading the horses and making sure they were comfortable in their stables Allen Smith and Lorraine went off together, clearly preoccupied with each other. Rachel didn't mind at all. She was always content on her own. One day she might be asked to ride at Chesterfield so she wanted to familiarise herself with the amenities for riders and stable staff and then walk the course. There was no substitute for that kind of homework, Mr Huzzard had impressed on her. A walk round the track was the only way of finding out where the little hollows and ridges were (for no racecourse was entirely flat) and how steep the camber was on tight bends. So far she had ridden in only two races, both of them at Market Rasen, an attractive small course in Lincolnshire. On each occasion she walked the course before riding it and thus learned a lot. Sadly, it hadn't helped her to gain a place. The horses she rode were not up to winning anything at that stage and so were complete outsiders. Still, the guv'nor had said he was pleased with her style and coolness and the fact that she hadn't made an obvious mistake at any point in the race. 'From someone with your experience, I couldn't ask more than that,' he told her; and she cherished his words.

Both those races were for amateur riders and her ambition was to compete with professionals. When that would happen she had no idea but she was well aware that trainers were chary of putting up amateurs against top jockeys, unless it was simply because the owner didn't want to have to pay a riding fee (amateur riders weren't paid; they were supposed to ride for the sheer pleasure of it). One day, though, it *would* happen and she intended to be ready for it.

Apart from problems associated with that short finishing stretch the Chesterfield course served up other tricky problems. The first bend was exceptionally sharp and any bunching at that point could result in trouble. Two of the hurdles on the back straight came very close together so it was necessary to have your horse positioned exactly right to jump them without risk of losing momentum. Horses which took the first one in their stride could be disconcerted by the suddenness with which they had to jump another obstacle. So, plainly, a jockey had to know what he was doing.

'Hey, don't know you – what're you riding?'

Rachel was so lost in her own thoughts that she hadn't noticed the figure overtaking her on the inside (that metaphor only struck her later). He was wearing a smart raincoat over his woollen colours and breeches. She guessed that meant he was riding in the first race.

'Er, I'm not,' she explained. 'Just – just planning for the future.'

'Good thinking,' he responded and fell into step beside her.

She enjoyed the chat and the friendliness. Sometimes racing seemed to her to be a rather ruthless world where people were only concerned about money and winning and really very little else. Kindness and interest in other people's welfare did not play a part. She realised as soon as the man introduced himself as Jake Cooper that he was a leading amateur rider and that he had the mount on the probable favourite in the first. He, too, he explained, hadn't previously ridden at Chesterfield.

'I think,' he said rather solemnly, 'you really need to know what you're doing on this track. Otherwise you and the horse will be taken by surprise – and the owner will be furious. To say nothing of the trainer!'

'Exactly!' Rachel agreed, and they both laughed.

After they parted by the weighing-room, where the jockeys would soon be assembling for the first, Rachel went off to the stables again to see that Catch Boy was still happy with life.

She knew she was tending to fuss over him as she gave his already gleaming coat another brushing but she preferred to spend her time with him. Horses, she was positive, were just like most humans in that they enjoyed a bit of company when in strange surroundings. Rachel had brought some food from the self-service cafeteria so she was able to have her lunch with him as well. She daren't, though, give him any titbits this time in case, however innocently, she infringed the rules of racing. The authorities were very strict about what could be fed to a horse before racing; and after its race a horse might have to be tested in a routine way to discover whether it had recently consumed any banned substances.

'So you see, Boy, we can't risk getting you in deep trouble,' she told him as he nuzzled yet again into her pocket.

She broke off in time to see the first race. Jake Cooper, riding a rather washy chestnut called Instantly, gained ground steadily between the last two sets of hurdles and even at that stage there wasn't much doubt he was going to be concerned in the finish. He still hadn't asked his horse for a real effort and yet he was closing fast on the two leaders who'd

been matching strides for some way. Instantly, as Rachel had noted, was a warm favourite and the crowd began to cheer him home as he approached the final hurdle. He clipped it so hard he knocked it out of the ground yet that hardly seemed to affect his momentum at all. After no more than a slap down the neck from his rider, Instantly swept into the lead and won comfortably.

To Rachel that seemed a very good omen for the chances of Catch Boy, though she realised there was no logic in her thinking. All the same, luck in racing often ran in cycles and she felt that luck was on her side at present.

Kevin Huzzard turned up with Allen Smith as the time drew near for Catch Boy's race. Rachel had half-expected that Bryn McWilliam would be with them and she was rather relieved that he wasn't. Bryn would undoubtedly have made some sarcastic comment about her. As it was the guv'nor and his head lad expressed satisfaction with the horse's appearance and placid demeanour.

'You'd hardly know he wasn't at home, he looks so relaxed,' Mr Huzzard remarked. 'Well done, Rachel. You're obviously good for him wherever he is.'

They ran practised hands over his legs to check that he hadn't suffered any knocks while travelling. Then he was saddled up and rugged in readiness for the parade ring.

'Quite happy about taking him round?' Allen inquired.

'Oh, of course!' she replied with such force that both men laughed. She was never quite sure about Allen's sense of humour or even whether he really possessed one.

The walk round and round the parade ring with the rest of the runners in single file could sometimes be an ordeal. This appearance in public, with crowds of people leaning over the rails to study them, could upset some horses, stir them up so that they became not only frisky but occasionally even a danger to the other animals. Then there were always some members of the public who passed unkind or supposedly witty comments on various horses or even their handlers.

'By, that 'un looks fit!' a man in a thick sheepskin coat exclaimed as Catch Boy went past him. 'Is he going to win, love?' he demanded of Rachel.

Most handlers, she knew, had been warned never to enter into conversation with strangers at racecourses, especially when in charge of their horse in the parade ring. But Rachel didn't think she would be doing any harm in smiling at the man and saying enthusiastically: 'We hope so!' After all, it was the truth and surely applied to the connections of every runner.

Catch Boy, well aware that something special was going on, kept leaning on her and she had to push back into his shoulder to prevent herself being knocked into the rail. Lots of horses had that trick and the effort of controlling the horse took a lot out of the handler. 'Feels like you've been in a gigantic wrestling match,' Nicola once remarked. Rachel agreed. The worst part of the battle came when another runner entered the ring just in front of you, and you then had to stop your horse from walking on until the newcomer could be slotted into the carousel.

Rachel wondered if Nicola was well enough to watch the race on television. At least that way she'd be able to see how Catch Boy got on. In fact, she'd probably see more of the actual race than Rachel would. Rachel wasn't aware of the presence of the cameras although she'd noticed them earlier. All her attention now was given to her horse and to wondering what would happen to him during the race.

Five

Owners, trainers and jockeys entered the parade ring and keenly watched their own runners. A tall man in a grey trilby and elegant blue suit listening to Kevin Huzzard was Richard Cayley, Catch Boy's owner. Although she'd seen him in the yard a couple of times Rachel hadn't so far been introduced to him. But, like every other owner, he was looking at his horse, not the handler. 'What are his chances?' would be the vital question for the trainer. Well, Rachel knew Catch Boy wasn't expected to win but perhaps he wasn't a complete outsider. The clear favourite was Yachtsman, who had won his only previous race by the proverbial 'street'. Another bay with a very bouncy stride, Yachtsman looked fit; but not, in her opinion, as handsome as her horse.

When the call was made for the jockeys to mount, Rachel led Catch Boy into the centre of the ring where his rug was swiftly stripped off by Mr Huzzard. Bryn McWilliam was given a leg up into the saddle by the trainer as Catch Boy patiently awaited his rider.

Rachel was thankful that Boy was in such a placid mood. Occasionally horses played up furiously as they were about to be united with the jockey and it was always the stable lad or lass who had the difficult job of controlling and quietening the horse. Trainers tended to look askance at them as if it was the lad who was personally responsible for such displays of indiscipline. Mostly it was just nerves twanging as racetime came nearer and nearer. Horses sensed the added excitement affecting connections and crowd.

Bryn didn't deign to speak to her as she led Boy round the ring for his final circuit before being asked to canter down to the start. But he nodded as Rachel at last released the horse at the gate and called to him, 'Good luck!'

It was in her mind, though, that Catch Boy was the one who most needed luck so that he shouldn't suffer at the hands of his jockey. She would keep her fingers crossed that he returned calm and unscathed. Well, he would hardly be *calm*; any race excited a horse to some extent. With some hyper-sensitive types, it took hours for them to return to normality. Then, to her astonishment, she heard her own name being announced over the public address system.

'The prize of £25 for the best turned-out horse has been awarded to No. 4, Catch Boy, who is looked after by Rachel Rastrick. Congratulations to them! The racecourse stewards are grateful for the sponsorship of A-to-Z Products PLC, who have donated this prize.'

'Goodness,' Rachel said, hardly aware that she was speaking aloud, however quietly, 'what a lovely surprise.' Her next thought was that it was really Nicola who deserved the prize. After all, Nicola had prepared Boy for his racecourse appearance before Rachel took over that morning.

Moments later she heard her name being called again.

'Mr Cayley, this is Rachel Rastrick, standing in as I told you for Nicola,' Kevin Huzzard said unexpectedly as Rachel was about to pass him with Boy's rug tucked under her arm. 'Rachel's already ridden a couple of races for me and is very keen to become a jockey one day.'

In the politest fashion, Catch Boy's owner raised his grey hat to her and inclined his head. He didn't, however, offer to shake hands.

'Congratulations on winning the prize,' he said suavely. 'The horse certainly looks very well, Rachel.'

'Thank you, Mr Cayley,' Rachel murmured. 'But I think Nicola deserves the credit.'

She wished afterwards that he'd said something about giving her a ride on one of his horses, especially Catch Boy. But that, she knew, was hardly likely yet. At least Mr Huzzard had made a point of introducing her. That counted for a lot. Well, it would if Richard Cayley bothered to remember her name.

By now the runners were milling round at the start before being called into line to face the tape and then

the two miles of the race. She would have preferred to push her way up the spectator-packed steps of the grandstand to see the race from a vantage point. Instead, she took her place on an ancient staircase close to the running-rail so as to be ready to re-possess her horse after the race. If it finished in the first three then she'd have to lead it into the winner's enclosure and stay with it until all the ceremonies were over and the horses could be removed to the privacy of their boxes. Standing with the lads, she wouldn't see as much of the race as she wanted to and she'd have to

rely on the racecourse commentary for significant
changes that occurred out of sight.

Muscles in her stomach were tightening even before the commentator announced: 'They're off!'
Standing and watching was much worse than actually
riding in the race. At this point she'd be concentrat-
ing on settling Catch Boy and ensuring he didn't take
too strong a hold. She wouldn't be aware of her own
emotions and tension.

A mare called Windfall was the first to show ahead
and there was no mention of Catch Boy before the

first hurdle was reached. Rachel approved of that omission. She had no idea how Bryn intended to ride the race, or what instructions he'd had from Kevin Huzzard, but she knew it wouldn't suit the bay to be pushed along too soon. He liked to get used to what was going on around him; but then, he wouldn't want to be held up too long, either.

Bryn would have to judge matters very carefully. If, Rachel told herself, he cared enough to do that. To him, this would be just another race, simply part of the day's work. To her, a ride on Catch Boy would be a dream come true. There was really no other way of describing such an experience.

The runners were now coming past the stands and Rachel craned her head for a better view. She knew Boy's gold-and-blue colours as well as she knew her favourite dress; and they sprang towards her from the middle of the bunch behind the two leaders. For Windfall was only half-a-length ahead of the favourite, Yachtsman. She watched intently as Catch Boy lobbed past her, going as easily as anyone could wish. Bryn was sitting quite still, plainly content to let Boy run his own race for the moment. Rachel couldn't fault that.

But the stable lad beside her was not at all pleased with his charge. 'Go *on*, you old sod, get going!' he yelled in the direction of a rather flashy chestnut at the very rear of the field. 'Go on, Craig, give the old devil a couple of whacks to waken him up properly.' If Craig, the jockey, heard that advice he didn't respond as directed. The hand holding the whip remained attached to the reins.

As the field swung leftwards into the first bend Yachtsman's impatience came to the fore; and thus it took him to the front. That was just what the commentator had been waiting for since the race began. Delightedly he was able to tell his listeners: 'And now Yachtsman's sailing along in front, leaving the others in his wake.' Several people got the joke and dutifully laughed. Almost immediately Catch Boy, too, made a forward move. Bryn had decided to see what Mr Cayley's bay was capable of now that the pace had increased.

One of the back-markers with the odd name of That Must Be Mine also started to weave his way through the field. So, suddenly, a race was developing. For the moment, though, Yachtsman was the unchallenged leader with Windfall three lengths behind. Catch Boy at that point was disputing third place with a grey called Island Mist. All the time, however, That Must Be Mine was making steady progress without being under any great pressure from his jockey. Inevitably, it was jockeyship that interested Rachel when she could spare the time from watching Catch Boy. She had thoroughly absorbed Kevin Huzzard's dictum that you never stopped learning about horses and how to ride 'em, not even if you were champion jockey. The thing never to forget was that no two horses were alike. Each must be treated as an individual.

Down the back straight Yachtsman actually increased his lead. Already the bookies were calling out that the leader was an odds-on chance. In fact, none of them wanted another penny on him despite offering that price.

'Come on, Boy, come on – time to close up,' Rachel urged under her breath.

She had observed, as perhaps Bryn had not, that the rangy chestnut That Must Be Mine was quickening dramatically. In a moment or two he would be disputing the lead with Yachtsman. If those two drew well ahead then it might be impossible for anyone else to get in a blow. A jockey, as she knew from even her limited experience, could wait too long before deciding to throw down a challenge.

Bryn was still biding his time, though it was clear to Rachel that Boy wanted to race. She winced as she saw how he was pulling the horse's head back to restrain him. They had already jumped the first of the two hurdles that were placed so close together. Catch Boy had been perfectly fluent at that one but now it was plain he was in two minds about how to jump the second. One moment his rider was restraining him, the next he was urging the horse to leap – and giving him a sharp reminder to do so.

Rachel screwed up her face in dismay as, through her binoculars, she saw exactly how Catch Boy reacted to such crass treatment. Instead of taking another half-stride before jumping, he took off instantaneously, hit the top of the hurdle and sprawled

awkwardly. It was, Rachel realised, a miracle that he hadn't fallen. As it was, Bryn lost one of his irons and tilted precariously out of the saddle. He might just have managed to stay on board if That Must Be Mine, still making relentless headway, hadn't cannoned into Boy's hindquarters. Inevitably, Bryn was catapulted from his perch but, luckily for him, he landed well clear of any galloping hooves.

Astonishingly, both horses appeared to have survived the mêlée unscathed. That Must Be Mine, after simply throwing up his head and shaking it once, resumed his challenge for the leadership; and Catch Boy, freed from the burden and threat of his rider, cantered after the rest of the field at his own steady pace. Already an ambulance was making its bumpy way towards the scene of the incident. However, after automatically noting that Bryn was on his feet again, Rachel kept her attention on Boy. Her remaining fear was that he would catch a foreleg in the dangling reins and trip himself up.

Serenely, Yachtsman continued to lead the field, unaware of the misfortune that had befallen one of his rivals. For a time it looked as though That Must Be Mine would offer the greatest threat to the favourite's supremacy but, just before the final obstacle, he seemed to run out of steam and faded quickly to finish only fifth. So Yachtsman won like the good thing all the punters had believed him to be. Rachel, of course, scarcely knew what had won: she had eyes only for Catch Boy and, to her intense relief, he trotted through the ranks of the sweating finishers looking as cool and sound as ever. She ran out to meet him and lead him back to the unsaddling area.

Kevin Huzzard was grim-faced and said nothing as he came up to check whether the horse had suffered any injuries, however slight; and Mr Cayley, equally silent, looked on as they waited for the return of their unseated jockey. As was customary in such circumstances, Bryn had got a lift back in the ambulance that had gone to his aid. He actually looked almost chirpy as he joined the group standing beside his recent partner, now rugged and comforted.

'So, what do you say happened out there, Bryn?' Mr Huzzard inquired curtly.

'Well, it must have been obvious to everyone, guv'nor,' Bryn began blithely. Then, remembering that the owner was present he quickly added a deferential 'Sir' and touched his cap. 'That bloke who barged into me must be a maniac, hasn't a clue how to handle a horse. My fella had jumped all wrong – told you he's still a big baby – but I could have got away with it if that idiot hadn't knocked me over. No chance of staying on board after that. Sorry, but there it is, guv'nor – sir. Lucky I wasn't murdered by the rest of the field galloping right over me.'

'Catch Boy jumped the previous hurdle perfectly,' Mr Cayley pointed out quietly. 'What was wrong with the next one?'

'He just didn't seem to know what to do, sir – took it all wrong. Came up a bit fast for him, I expect. As I said, sir, he's a bit raw, got a lot to learn about the jumping game.'

Mr Huzzard's eyes narrowed but, surprisingly, he didn't say anything. It was Rachel who spoke next, completely to her own surprise.

'Have you actually ridden round Chesterfield before, Bryn?'

The look he shot at her was made up of anger and astonishment; and as she saw it she suddenly realised what a mistake she'd made.

'Er, no,' Bryn answered bleakly. 'But I've watched plenty of racing here on the telly. I do know the course, you know.'

She'd intended to present him with an easy excuse for the error he'd made between the close-together hurdles. Instead, as she realised too late, it appeared that she'd been pointing out his lack of preparation for the race.

'Not quite the same thing, is it, young man?' Mr Cayley remarked coolly. 'Telly, as you call it, is an image: knowing a track from personal experience is the reality.'

As the owner turned away and began to move towards the stands Mr Huzzard acted swiftly to defuse what he recognised was a dangerous situation.

'Better get off and change for the next race, Bryn. Try to forget about this race and think about how to handle Hipperholme. And you, Rachel, take Catch Boy back to the stables and stay with him. He looks fine now but he's had a bit of a shock so we don't know how it'll affect him till he's home and tucked up in his own box again. Off you go then.'

Rachel tried to catch Bryn's eye and offer at least a token apology. But he strode away without another word. Not once had he so much as glanced at Catch Boy let alone given him a sympathetic pat. Perhaps, she reflected, he believed that the horse was at least partly responsible for his being decanted from the saddle. Bryn, being Bryn, would never blame himself for any fault at all.

So, of course, *he* wasn't to blame when Hipperholme failed to finish in the first three in the next race. Yet the novice chaser had been going beautifully until his jockey had urged him strenuously to the front between the last two fences.

Hipperholme was basically lazy and as soon as he struck the front he thought he'd done enough work for the day. So he stopped. Bryn was supposed to know all about that trick. But, in his eagerness to redeem his reputation after the disaster with Catch Boy, he failed to time Hipperholme's effort properly. And despite the application of a couple of hard cracks with the whip Hipperholme refused to exert himself again; indeed, he so resented the treatment he gave up galloping and dropped back to fourth place. For which, as everyone connected with a racing stable knew to their cost, there was no prize money (well, not for minor races, anyway).

Bryn's explanation to the unhappy trainer was that Hipperholme 'simply blew up – he's just not fit enough yet to get the trip'.

Rachel, who'd faithfully followed instructions to stay with Catch Boy, only heard about Bryn's comment when the stable's two runners were being prepared for the return journey to Mintonbury Magna. Even their current affection for each other couldn't prevent Allen Smith and Lorraine from being thoroughly despondent about the afternoon's results.

'Honestly, I think the guv'nor's luck is dead out,' the head lad remarked in the gloomiest tones to his girlfriend and Rachel. 'If it doesn't alter soon we'll be in real trouble. Then there'll have to be changes – even if owners don't start taking their horses away to other trainers. And if *that* happens we'll definitely be on the slippery slope to disaster.'

Six

The depression hanging over Kevin Huzzard's racing stables hadn't lifted by the following morning when Rachel arrived to help out as usual. In fact, it seemed to be even deeper for it was plainly affecting everyone who worked there. None of the lads or lasses could summon up a grin let alone a friendly word of greeting. Even Allen was snapping at people for no apparent reason: just the clatter of a dropped brush could arouse his anger. If such a mood, and its attendant tensions, persisted then the horses themselves would quickly sense it and become nervous or uncooperative.

Much to Rachel's surprise, Nicola was already at work, mucking out Catch Boy's box. Boy pricked his ears and moved forward immediately to greet Rachel but Nicola promptly shoved him back unceremoniously.

'Oh, hello, Nicola. Good to see you. How are you?'

'Right enough,' the other girl muttered. 'Look, what've you done with the money?'

'Money?' Rachel was totally baffled.

'Yeah, the 25 quid for best-turned out horse yesterday. That should be mine, you know. I did everything except take the horse to the races, so I deserve the prize.'

'Oh, well, yes, I suppose so. But, you see, Mr Huzzard said the fairest thing was to put it into the prize money fund for the lads to share out at Christmas – you know, so that everybody gets something extra.'

'Including you!'

Rachel was taken aback by the bitterness of that comment and didn't know what to answer. She wasn't the slightest bit interested in the money but Nicola wasn't likely to believe that.

'Look, Catch Boy's *my* horse, so don't go thinking he's yours and you can do what you like with him,' Nicola went on forcefully. 'I saw the way you were petting him yesterday in the parade ring – I watched everything on the telly. If you hadn't got him so relaxed and soft he might have won. Horses need gee-ing up when they've got to race. You remember that, Razzy.'

However, Rachel was given the leg-up on Catch Boy to ride out on the gallops. As was the case with all the stable lads, Nicola 'did' two horses and, of course, she couldn't ride both when they went out at the same time. So she was in charge of Zygomatic, yet another of the stable's temperamental inhabitants (Allen Smith had once aired the view that racing's odd-ball horses always finished up in the smallest and poorest stables because none of the main training establishments would tolerate them). Zygomatic definitely possessed ability but he rarely consented to show it. On the gallops he wouldn't work at all unless he had another horse on either side of him, stationed more or less at his girths. Nicola undeniably got on with him better than any one and so it was inevitable that Allen should have listed her to ride him that morning.

Catch Boy, at least, was in good spirits as the string filed out of the yard and headed for the gallops on the Downs just above the town. Clearly he was none the worse for his mishap at Chesterfield and Rachel had discreetly checked that there weren't any blemishes on his flanks as a result of his collision with That Must Be Mine. He was stepping out in the jauntiest style and Rachel had to keep him in check. She didn't want to attract any more unfavourable comments from the other riders, every one of whom was in an unusually silent mood. Allen and Lorraine weren't exchanging so much as a word.

It was a crisp, blue-sky morning with a sharp wind and because it was Sunday more people were about than was usual on a weekday morning. Dogs were being exercised and that was always a worry for the riders; if some belligerent poodle sounded off near them some horses quickly displayed nervousness and a desire to get well clear of that spot. Idly, Rachel noticed that on the far side of the broad stretch of turf used for the gallops someone was practising his golf swing. She was thankful no one was flying a kite. That was guaranteed to upset all but the calmest animals.

Because serious work was rarely done on the gallops on a Sunday Kevin Huzzard tended to remain at the stables and leave his head lad in charge. Allen Smith had given his orders, and Rachel was waiting to accompany Tracey Sterling (riding another novice hurdler called Kippford) on a five-furlong spin, when suddenly a horse gave a strangled sort of squeal and reared steeply. In almost the same moment a golf ball bounced up beside Rachel almost at shoulder height. But the bouncing ball was only a momentary distraction: for the horse that had reared was now back on four legs and charging away across the Downland towards the path that led directly into the town. It was Packed Lunch, the mount of Cheryl, now prone on the ground after being thrown. Lorraine was already dismounting from her own horse to go and attend to Cheryl.

Rachel didn't hesitate. Packed Lunch had to be caught before he caused damage to himself or anyone or anything he encountered in his headlong flight. A runaway horse was the fear of every stable for the trouble it could cause was incalculable: and a racehorse running wild in a town centre, or on a highway, was a nightmare.

Catch Boy's acceleration was swift. He had been ready for a gallop and so he was going to enjoy it. The fact that he was being sent in a different direction from usual didn't bother him at all. Rachel, confident in her relationship with the horse, was sure that he'd respond to whatever she asked of him. How she was going to recapture Packed Lunch she had no idea. Her sole ambition for the moment was simply to catch up with him before disaster struck.

By now Packed Lunch was out of sight. He had disappeared down the narrowing strip of turf that gave way eventually to tarmacadam and then joined the gentle hill into the town centre of Mintonbury. It occurred to her that Packed Lunch might well pull himself up by the old fence on the edge of the Downs if he veered away from the roadway: on the other hand, as a practised jumper he could just as easily take it in his stride. She doubted whether anyone in his right senses would attempt to stop the runaway; most people, though, took fright at the sight of a charging horse even if they were quite used to handling horses under controlled circumstances.

Catch Boy seemed to know that he was giving chase – even though he couldn't possibly have sight of their quarry. He was racing with great freedom and reacted immediately Rachel gave him an instruction: left a little here, slow there, go on, go on! They swept past a startled young couple, who pointed speechlessly towards the gap in the fence by a cluster of trees. Rachel waved that she understood what they were telling her but didn't waste breath on words. It was obvious that Packed Lunch was still travelling at speed. The young couple had clearly had a shock.

Boy slithered on a deep patch of damp leaves and Rachel had to check him. One of the worst things that could happen now would be for *them* to run into trouble.

Then they reached the road. A car coming up the hill had stopped and the driver was craning his neck out of the window to see what was going on behind him. Out of sight another vehicle was blowing its horn and Rachel prayed that didn't mean there'd already been an accident. But the sound of the horn was likely further to alarm the distressed Packed Lunch.

Rachel had never travelled at such speed on horse-back on a metalled road. But she had no sense of fear at all. Really, the whole experience so far had been exhilarating. Her faith in him was boundless. Another car emerged from a side entrance and instantly braked as the driver glimpsed her furious approach. Another passer-by, deducing her purpose, pointed and shouted.

'It's cutting across the market place, that horse — nearly knocked a child down! Go steady, for the Lord's sake!'

The he turned and shakily climbed the steps of a Primitive Methodist chapel, whose double doors weren't even open yet.

At last, on the far side of the partly-cobbled square, she spotted Packed Lunch again. He was turning sharply by the plate-glass window of a fashion store, turning in bewilderment and despair. It was a miracle he hadn't gone through the glass: and if he had that would have been the end of him, Rachel had no doubt. For a moment, he was stationary, unable to see a route to freedom. Two frightened pedestrians were cowering in a shop doorway but they were in less danger than the two cars parked at the pavement's edge in front of the fashion store. Packed Lunch had already eyed them like a prospective hurdle he might have to jump.

Nobody was going to approach the terrified chestnut. ... except Rachel.

She had slowed Catch Boy down to a walk and now, as they crossed the square, she wondered whether to dismount. But if Packed Lunch bolted again she'd lose valuable seconds getting back into the saddle. By now all traffic had come to a halt, awaiting the outcome of Rachel's approach to the runaway horse. She felt like a matador in a bull ring: but she was trying to placate an animal, not provoke one. Spectators gawped or held their breath.

Packed Lunch noisily scraped a hoof across a flagstone and gave her an uncertain look. She sensed then that he was going to run again, and she was right. The chestnut turned and dived down an alleyway, his hooves now skittering on the shining cobblestones. Someone in the throng of watchers in a doorway had moved suddenly and that was enough to alarm him again. Rachel, however, felt more hopeful of success: for the alleyway, as she well knew, was a cul-de-sac. Packed Lunch couldn't possibly get out at the other

end.

She dismounted and stationed Catch Boy across the entrance to the alleyway. She would have liked to ask someone to hold his head but everyone kept well back. She wanted Catch Boy to remain as still as a sentry in front of a royal palace. So she told him what she wanted and prayed he understood.

Slowly she walked along the alleyway, calling softly to the chestnut that everything was all right, that there was nothing to be scared of, that he'd soon be back in his own box and happy as a king. To her own ears much of it sounded a bit silly but it was necessary to reassure the horse. She passed a tiny betting shop

on the right and couldn't help wondering what the
punters would have thought had it been a weekday
and they'd seen a racehorse charging past their doorway. Doubtless some wit would have offered odds in
running!

Packed Lunch had taken refuge in a pub yard at
the very end of the alleyway. He backed away as he
heard her approach and bumped against a barrel.
Luckily it didn't fall over for the noise would probably have put him to flight again. His ears, she saw,
were pricked, not laid back. That was the best sign
yet that she might succeed in recapturing him. Her
voice, and the gentleness of her manner, were begin-

ning to calm him.

As she drew nearer she spread her arms wide to discourage any ideas he had about making a break for it. Normally, no horse would charge straight into a person; it would to its utmost to avoid a collision. Packed Lunch's ears quivered again and he tried to back away until his haunches came firmly into contact with the back wall of the pub.

'Rest-a-bit, rest-a-bit. Easy, boy, easy,' she murmured. He knew her voice and the fear began to leave his eyes. 'Come on, now, it's all over – the trouble's all over. There are no more golf balls flying around here.'

Instinctively she knew that Packed Lunch had been hit by the ball that she saw bouncing beside her on the Downs. It had ricocheted from Lunch's flanks after being caught by a swirl of wind. That stupid golfer should be prosecuted, she told herself. He could have caused a major catastrophe.

Packed Lunch surrendered quite easily in the end. He allowed her to catch hold of his bridle and then very carefully lead him out of the yard and back down the alleyway. A small crowd had crept forward to see the drama unfolding and several people were a bit disappointed that the excitement was all over. Rachel was keeping her fingers crossed that they wouldn't start clapping or cheering or do anything that would startle the horse afresh. Now that he was under control she wasn't going to lose him at any cost.

Then coming towards her she saw Kevin Huzzard.

He looked like a man who'd just been told he wasn't to face the firing squad after all.

'Rachel, thank goodness you're both safe! They told me what had happened and I dashed down here in the car. I honestly thought I was going to find mayhem. You must have done wonderfully well to settle him down after what happened. Wonderfully.'

'It was easier than I thought it was going to be,' Rachel replied truthfully. 'And Catch Boy was a great help. He did everything asked of him just perfectly.'

She wasn't sure the trainer was listening. He was making the most careful examination of Packed Lunch's legs and belly to see that he'd suffered no injuries.

'It's an absolute miracle that he's come to no harm,' he murmured in disbelief. 'A miracle.'

The reporter from the local paper was not quite so impressed when he turned up at Mintonbury Magna stables that afternoon to interview Rachel Rastrick, the town's 'pretty young heroine' as the headline-writer was to describe her. He treated the story in a very matter-of-fact fashion, perhaps because it hadn't ended in a welter of blood and gore after all. He preferred melodrama to miraculous misses.

Rachel, as she reluctantly posed for yet another camera shot, was quite pleased that the whole thing was being played down at last. Kevin Huzzard had continued to make a fuss of her when they all returned to the stables and the other stable girls were friendlier than they'd ever been. Cheryl, fortunately, had come to no harm either, as a result of being thrown, but she'd been sent home for a rest as a precaution. One major regret was that nobody had thought to apprehend the amateur golfer and point out to him the trouble he'd caused. But perhaps the reporter would do that for them, in print.

By early afternoon Rachel was thankful to have the place to herself, for that was what it felt like when Mr Huzzard had retired to his house to do paperwork and the rest of the staff were off duty until evening stables. She was delaying her visit to Catch Boy's box because that would add to the pleasure of the time she'd spend with him. In any case, he'd already been fussed over enough that day for, of course, if she was the heroine then he was definitely the hero. There were plenty of jobs to do around the stable and one of her discoveries was the tiny puncture marks on Hipperholme's belly, caused by sharp twigs when hitting the top of a fence. So she made a note that poultices and antibiotics would be needed to clear up that little problem.

It was just as she was about to leave the tack room, where she'd been checking for worn stirrup leathers, that Bryn McWilliam turned up. The stable jockey wasn't normally to be found there on a Sunday afternoon but he'd called in simply to use the hose pipe on his car. He was genuinely startled to find Rachel in the tack room.

'Still greasing round the guv'nor to get what you

want, I see,' he said challengingly when he'd recovered from the surprise.

'If that's what you see then you've got very funny eyes,' Rachel replied coolly, wondering how she was going to get past him and out of the room before he said anything worse.

'There was nothing *funny* about what you said at Chesterfield yesterday,' he said savagely. 'That sort of rotten trick could get me the chop from an owner like Mr Cayley. But I expect that's what you want – to get *my* rides. To take the bread out of my mouth!'

'You don't eat bread,' she pointed out. 'You say it puts on weight.'

As soon as she'd spoken those words she wished she hadn't. She felt she'd antagonised him enough already. And, after all, she had inadvertently put him in a difficult position with her remark about walking the course.

But before she could phrase an apology he suddenly swooped towards her. For a moment, she thought he was going to attack her; then, to her amazement, she realised he was trying to kiss her. He succeeded once before she managed to push him off. Her strength surprised him.

'Come on,' he said thickly, grabbing her again, 'you know I've always fancied you.'

Rachel, reacting instinctively this time, slapped him across the face.

Bryn staggered back against the wall, dislodging some stirrup irons that fell to the floor with a con-

siderable clatter.

'Makes a change for somebody to hit *you*, doesn't it?' she said, and then darted past him and out into the yard.

He bounced up off the wall and came charging after her. 'You stupid little schoolgirl. I'll – '

The yell died in his throat as he saw Kevin Huzzard striding towards them.

'What's going on between you two?' the trainer wanted to know. The red mark on Bryn's cheek was plainly visible. 'Are you having a row or something?'

'Er, well, sort of,' Bryn muttered, not having the faintest idea what to say to defuse the situation. He looked desperately towards Rachel.

'It's my fault,' she admitted. 'Bryn was mad at me for what I said yesterday about not walking the course. I should have apologised sooner. I'd no right to make that remark. So, sorry, Bryn.'

'Oh, er, that's all right, Raz,' Bryn had the good sense to reply, while still looking surprised. 'Let's forget it.'

Kevin Huzzard, glancing curiously from one to the other and not at all taken in by such a show of concern for other people's feelings, decided to take no action apart from issuing a general warning about future conduct.

'We have enough problems in this stable without people falling out with each other, so try to remember that. If there's a bad atmosphere in the yard then it's the horses that suffer first, then the owners and me

81

most of all. Just think about that. O.K.?'

They nodded in unison. Then Bryn explained that he'd only dropped in to wash his car and so he'd go and get on with it. Mr Huzzard nodded his approval of that diplomatic withdrawal and then turned to Rachel.

'Right, young lady, I think you've earned a rest after completing all your good deeds for the day,' he said briskly. 'But before you go you might like to know I've just been talking on the phone with Richard Cayley about the race yesterday. And he happened to mention that he thought you were a very composed and intelligent girl. Those were his exact words. I told him I agreed entirely.'

When, a few minutes later, Rachel went off to collect her bike for the ride home she felt as though she were walking on air.

Seven

Leaden was how Rachel would have described her feelings if anybody had asked her as, the following Saturday afternoon, she and her mother arrived at the Starlite Model Agency's studio. All her pleas and threats and conviction that the whole thing would be a complete waste of everybody's time and money had not made a scrap of difference to Mrs Rastrick's determination to go ahead with the photographic session she believed would be Rachel's first step on the short road to a successful modelling career. As a last resort Rachel had tried to enlist the support of Annajane to come along and pour gallons of icy water on the scheme. Annajane, however, had chosen that very afternoon to visit a friend in the physiotherapy department of the local hospital to pick up some vital practical tips that would help her own future career.

A girl who looked not much older than Rachel came forward to greet them. As she had two cameras slung from her neck she hardly needed to explain that she was a photographer. Her name was Lisa and

Rachel was marginally mollified that the pictures were to be taken by her. After all, another girl of about her own age ought to be able to understand her feelings on the subject of her true ambitions.

'I'm sure you'll enjoy it once you can relax,' Lisa tried to assure her as she adjusted lamps and back-cloths and fiddled with yet another camera on a tri-pod. 'I'll just take a few ordinary shots of you first before we see what you're like wearing different out-fits. O.K.?'

Rachel submitted to demands to turn this way, twist in that direction, hold this pose and lean that way, yes, just a tiny bit further, thank you – exactly, keep it like that, don't move! She was bored and it showed. Her mother's fierce shakes of the head to indicate disapproval of Rachel's attitude had no effect on her.

Lisa was too bright not to get the message. After another change of attire in which Rachel went leth-argically through what had become a familiar routine the photographer announced it was time for a break. She certainly looked as though she herself needed one; but then it had become very hot under the strong lights in the cramped studio.

'You're very thin, aren't you, though pretty strong, too, I imagine,' Lisa remarked conversa-tionally as they sipped the tea that had been ordered.

'But isn't that exactly what you want nowadays – the slim, sleek, schoolgirl look?' Mrs Rastrick in-quired sharply.

Lisa looked startled. 'Well, it, er, all depends,' she answered carefully. 'I'm really only the photographer. You'd have to ask Mr Lawrence. He's the boss and he knows what's in fashion.'

'Mr *Wolford* Lawrence?' asked Mrs Rastrick, looking surprised.

'That's right! You know him?'

'I used to. Oh, yes, I used to know him very well.'

There was a pause which was broken when Lisa, who had been looking puzzled, remarked to Rachel: 'You know, I'm sure I've seen you somewhere before – and recently. I'm good at faces – have to be – but terrible on names. Could swear I'd seen your picture in a magazine or some place like that.'

So Rachel told her about the story and picture that had appeared that week in the local paper about her rescue of Packed Lunch. It was actually on the front page and the photograph showed her face to face with Packed Lunch.

'Of course, how stupid of me to forget!' Lisa exclaimed, looking genuinely annoyed. 'Hey, that must have taken great courage to chase off like that. I know just what horses can be like when they're all stirred up. You see, I'm really keen on sports photography. That's why I notice the shots in the papers, even if I forget the names of the people in them!'

After that revelation the two girls chatted enthusiastically about racing and other equine topics. Rachel didn't have to explain about her hopes for the future; Lisa realised at once that she couldn't possibly contemplate any other ambition than to be a jockey.

Mrs Rastrick, ignored completely for several minutes, could stand the chatter no longer.

'Isn't it time?' she interrupted coldly. 'Time to get back to the business we're here for?'

'Oh, sure,' Lisa replied guiltily. 'Sorry to get carried away with the horses – if you see what I mean.'

For the first time that day Rachel laughed uninhibitedly.

But then, before even one more photograph could be taken, an office door opened and in walked a tall, elegantly dressed man with a distinguished air. He exchanged smiles with Lisa and Rachel and glanced across at Mrs Rastrick. As he did so, she rose to her feet, a look of surprise turning to delight spreading across her face.

'Wolford! Wolford, how wonderful to see you again. So unexpected, too.'

There was no doubt Mrs Rastrick meant what she was saying. Rachel couldn't remember seeing her mother's eyes glow like that.

The hesitation on his part was barely detectable.

'It's Deborah – Deborah Rastrick, isn't it? Good grief, what a surprise to see you. What brings *you* here?'

'My daughter, Rachel – she's here to be photographed, you see. We thought, well, modelling possibilities. *You* know. But I'd no idea, Wolford, you were still in the business.'

86

'How very extraordinary!' His glance at Rachel was brief. Then all his attention returned to her mother. 'After all these years, to meet like this, in my studio, of all places. Is she – Rachel, did you say – is she the child you were carrying when you had your change of heart?'

'Yes. My only child, as it's turned out.'

'Extraordinary,' Wolford Lawrence said again, clearly now gathering thoughts and memories. 'Did you ever take up modelling again later? Are you doing any now?'

Rachel was regarding her mother with astonishment as Mrs Rastrick shook her head. At no time had she ever confided to Rachel that she'd once been a

87

model, although it had been obvious that she had a passionate interest in fashion and modelling as a career. Lisa, too, was fascinated by the conversation and looking at Mrs Rastrick in a quite different way from five minutes earlier. It hadn't even occurred to her that she should still be taking photographs.

Suddenly, Mr Lawrence switched his attention to Rachel and smiled brightly.

'So, young lady, are you planning to follow in your mother's footsteps? he asked.

'I don't understand what you mean,' Rachel replied flatly. As she'd guessed it would, that answer caused Mr Lawrence to give her mother an inquiring look.

'I never told her, Wolford, because I didn't want to influence her unduly,' Mrs Rastrick said calmly. 'But now she knows something she might just as well know it all. Rachel, I was a model for a time and I enjoyed it. I intended to go on and have a wonderful career. Mr Lawrence here was very encouraging, very helpful. But just when everything was about to take off for me I found I was pregnant. Your father and I desperately wanted a child so we agreed straight away that I should give up modelling. In any case, I should have had to give it up as I put on weight. Then you were born and that was that. I wanted to be with you all the time as you grew up. And I was. I've – I've never regretted that for a moment.'

Rachel was flabbergasted. Never had such a story even been hinted at before today. It ended all her speculation about her own identity. Clearly, Deborah Rastrick *was* her mother!

After that revelation there was a brief silence. It was broken when Mr Lawrence turned back to Rachel and asked her again if she wanted a career in modelling.

'Not in the slightest,' Rachel said firmly.

'I think perhaps that's wise of you because – ' he was saying when Mrs Rastrick interrupted.

'Wolford, please explain to her what a glorious opportunity she's throwing away! A once-in-a-lifetime opportunity. At her age, with all the attributes she has. . . .'

'Well, Deborah, I don't think that's strictly true in Rachel's case. I must be honest – you know I've never been one to mislead anybody about something as vital as a career – so I have to say that girls with the build and the looks of Rachel are simply not in demand at present.'

He paused and when no one else spoke he added: 'Quite frankly, pretty though you undoubtedly are Rachel, I'm afraid your slim, rather boyish figure is just not in fashion, literally. It's the fuller, mature figure, that I'm looking for as a model. *Your* kind of figure, Deborah, with your exquisite hands, which are always so important to a model. Now if only you were available I could provide you with all the work you wanted, and more, believe me.'

'There you are, Mum, you've got a second chance,' Rachel said triumphantly. 'So, go on, take it.'

'I really wish you would,' said Mr Lawrence with a grateful glance at Rachel.

Mrs Rastrick had been looking non-plussed. But she recovered quickly.

'I'll think about it,' she said thoughtfully. 'Yes, I'll definitely think about it. Because *you* have asked me, Wolford.'

'Please do, Deborah. Just give me a ring any time and I'll fix an appointment for you like a shot.'

Five minutes later, after Rachel and Lisa had sworn promises to keep in touch on sporting matters, Mrs Rastrick and her daughter left the Starlite Studio. Much to their surprise, they both experienced a sense of satisfaction about the visit.

'Well, you're going to get what you wanted, after all, Mum, even if it has been delayed a few years,' Rachel remarked as they got into the car for the drive home. 'And I'm going to get what *I* want. Nothing, and nobody, is going to stop me.'

Eight

When, nearly three weeks later, the telephone rang late on the Friday evening and Rachel's father told her the caller was Kevin Huzzard her mouth suddenly dried up with nervous excitement. For Catch Boy was due to run again at Chesterfield the following day.

'Got a ride for you at Chesterfield tomorrow, if you're interested,' the trainer greeted her with deliberate nonchalance.

'Oh, great, Mr Huzzard! Absolutely great! Is it – is it – '

'No, sorry, Ray, it isn't Catch Boy,' he cut in. 'Bryn's still down to partner him. No, this one is in the first race, the one for amateur riders. Horse called Hay Days, trained by Billy Allaway. Mr Cayley's got a couple of horses with him and I gather he was the one who recommended you to Billy. Seems this is a nice sort of a horse but just a wee bit headstrong. Been out a couple of times and finished unplaced, run out of steam most likely. The thinking is he might settle for a girl. So what do you say?'

'I'm delighted to accept – and very grateful to Mr Cayley.'

'Good, good. Well, it'll be useful experience for you whatever happens. Don't forget to bring your riding gear when you come in the morning. See you then. Sleep well, Rachel.'

It was, as she'd expected it to be, a long time before she got off to sleep. The initial disappointment that she was not to ride Catch Boy quickly gave way to excitement. Hay Days, she decided, was rather a happy name for a horse. She'd never heard of him before but that wasn't surprising because there were thousands of racehorses in training. As she was riding against fellow amateurs the competition shouldn't be so severe. If she made mistakes perhaps they wouldn't be as noticeable as they would in a race dominated by ambitious professional jockeys.

Her mother, on hearing the news, had even offered to drive to Chesterfield on her own to support her. Rachel, though grateful that her mother had at long last accepted her ambitions, thought that wasn't a good idea. If she had a crashing fall or made a calamitous error of judgment she didn't want any member of her family to observe it.

The following morning was moist and misty and Rachel's first fear was that racing at Chesterfield might be abandoned because of fog. She listened to weather reports on her transistor as she made breakfast but she learned little that helped to clarify the situation. In any case, local fog could disperse rapidly if the sun broke through and thus in such conditions no decision about an abandonment would be taken early.

By leaving home a few minutes earlier than usual, putting her head down and pedalling hard she managed to avoid an encounter at his gate with Mr Thornton. If her name was in the newspaper as the rider of Hay Days he'd be sure to quiz her in detail about its chances. He'd hardly believe that, at present, she almost certainly knew less about the horse than he did from his devoted study of the form book. On top of everything else, she felt she never had much luck on the days she met him.

At the stables she managed to spend a few minutes with Catch Boy while Nicola was with Zygomatic. Nicola had maintained a frosty attitude towards her for a week or so after the prize money incident but now they were on reasonably friendly terms again. It was Nicola's job to look after Catch Boy at Chesterfield and so Rachel could concentrate on preparing herself for the ride on Hay Days.

Allen Smith had noticed the booking and had some advice for her.

'Let him know who's boss right from the start. These unknown quantities can be right tearaways, so don't let him get up to any tricks. Keep a real tight hold of his head, especially on the way down to the start. Then you're likely to come back together, not in separate pieces.'

At the racecourse itself more advice was offered freely by various envious stable lads, other riders and, more importantly, by Hay Days' trainer, Billy Allaway, a jovial little man wearing an outsize trilby hat. He had a trick of clasping Rachel's wrist between his hands as he talked to her.

'He's not a bad little horse, this one, but he's a bit green,' he explained in an earnest manner. 'I think perhaps he wants the gentle touch, the soft voice, and I'm sure he'll get that with you, love. You're really pretty to look at and I'm sure you've got a big, kind heart. I think this little horse was knocked about a bit when he was young and so he's liable to get upset if folk sound cross. So just take things easy, all round, love. All right?'

That advice seemed to conflict with what she'd been told by Allen Smith but she had to forget that.

'Very good, Mr Allaway,' she said politely. 'I'll remember all that.'

Nothing was said about the owner of Hay Days so she assumed he wasn't present. Doubtless, though, he'd receive a full report from the trainer in due course on her handling of the horse: and that would surely determine whether she was ever offered another ride for the stable. The fluttering of nerves in her tummy wouldn't die down and she desperately wanted to nibble some food to calm herself. Even though she would have no weight problems whatsoever, for the horse was due to carry 10 st. 7 lbs. (which meant putting a lot of lead in the saddle pockets to make up the difference between that weight and Rachel's), she felt that it would be unwise to eat in view of her forthcoming exertions.

Many racecourses still hadn't adapted to the increasing numbers of women riders and so Rachel wasn't at all surprised to find that the ladies' changing facilities were in what was formerly a storeroom attached to the First Aid Room. Such a location didn't exactly help to settle the stomachs of nervous newcomers to the chasing game! One other girl was already in the room, and halfway through changing her clothes, but apart from an exchange of greetings she didn't seem to want to talk. Rachel was glad to discover that the room contained a wash-basin but, predictably, no shower; yet a shower was what she most enjoyed after a race whether or not the conditions had been muddy.

She ran her hands over the woollen jersey, knitted in the owner's colours of daffodil yellow, light blue and red, but before she put it on she tucked her back-protector into place. The vulnerable spine had to be protected if she suffered a fall and a horse kicked out or galloped over her. All being well, her specially-strengthened helmet would save her head from injury.

Before leaving the changing-room to go and weigh out she picked up her whip: although she'd vowed never to use it to hurt a horse it did help a rider's balance. There was an unfamiliar dryness in her mouth as she went through the ritual of sitting on the scales while clutching her saddle and then making her way to the paddock where the horses were already revolving. To her delight, Hay Days proved to be a very good-looking deep chestnut with three white socks and a particularly luxuriant mane. He was being led round by a young lad and Rachel couldn't help wondering how he'd reacted to the news that his charge was to be ridden by a girl, and an unknown girl at that.

Billy Allaway touched his hat to her as they met in the centre of the ring and that gesture impressed her greatly. After all, it was usually the jockey who responded in that way to the presence of owner and trainer.

'Feeling a touch nervous?' he inquired with one of his widest grins.

'A bit,' she admitted.

'Just as it should be, love. That way you won't get too cocky and think you know it all. Now, Rachel, just remember what I said: take it easy and come back safe and sound. Bringing the horse *with you*, of course!'

She was able to laugh at that and by the time he gave her a leg up into the saddle she was feeling quite relaxed. The lad smiled at her, too, and wished her the best of luck. Nobody had said anything at all about the prospect of winning or even gaining a place. So she was under no pressure at all to achieve something in particular.

In any case, Hay Days was a long-priced outsider.

The two disputing favouritism were Chapel Row and Vicksburg; the latter was ridden by the leading amateur, Jake Cooper whom Rachel had met on her previous visit to Chesterfield. A bay called Ever-so-helpful was trying to show he'd been ill-named by throwing his head about in a very wild manner as he left the paddock. Rachel was thankful her mount was so placid; it was undeniably embarrassing to have to fight for control in front of such a multitude of spectators.

The weather had improved, but only marginally, for there were still mist patches about and visibility from the grandstands would not be good. Ever-so-helpful had calmed down by the time the ten runners were called into line and, typically, he was now show-ing signs of not wanting to start at all. In fact, when the flag fell and the race began only Hay Days was eager to get into his stride. That was just what Rachel had expected from the form he'd displayed in pre-vious outings but she didn't see any point in restrain-ing him. They'd both lose a lot of energy that way. Moreover he wasn't trying to run away with her. He was simply moving freely and apparently enjoying the exercise. Clearly nobody else wanted to make the running and so Hay Days built up a good lead before he reached the first hurdle. And how he took that hurdle would be the first real test of their partnership.

The chestnut approached the obstacle with ears pricked and giving no indication at all that it worried him. Plainly, it didn't. For he skipped over it as if he'd been doing nothing else all his life. Literally, he took it in his stride. Rachel was overjoyed. She stretched forward to stroke his neck and shout: 'Well done, Hay Days, *well done*!'

Hay Days showed his gratitude for such praise by, if anything, increasing his pace. Yet she had no fear at all that he was exerting himself too much at this comparatively early stage of the race. Nor was he threatening to run away with her, as he might have tried to do were he not in control of himself. The apprehensions she'd held about riding in this race were vanishing with every stride. Already, she was beginning to enjoy herself. So, too, was Hay Days. There couldn't be any doubt about that even to the watchers in the stands.

The next two hurdles were jumped with the same fluency and by now Rachel was wondering how far ahead of the field they must be. No other runner had loomed up alongside them; and, more astonishing still, she couldn't even hear the sounds of hooves or the shouts of other riders. Normally no race was run in silence. Jockeys were forever yelling comments to each other or asking for room to get through when crowded out and in a challenging position. But she wasn't going to risk a glance over her shoulder. She'd been told often enough how unwise that could be, if only because of the effect it had on a jockey's concentration.

Even though they were now in the back straight,

heading for the two jumps that came so close together, the first sound she heard was made by the crowd: a collective gasp of disappointment as Vicksburg, the outright favourite at the 'off', made a complete hash of his attempt to clear an obstacle. As the horse sprawled and dropped a shoulder his rider, Jake Cooper, had no hope of staying in the saddle. Jake hit the ground, rolled into a ball to avoid as much trouble as possible and waited until the rest of the field had gone by before rising with a rueful smile. Vicksburg, quite unharmed, galloped on as though nothing had happened: and then, at the very next hurdle, veered sharply across the path of Chapel Row, whose rider almost had to pull his horse's head off to avoid a collision.

Completely unaware of this mini-mayhem behind her Rachel carried serenely on and approached the twin obstacles with confidence. It was entirely justified. Hay Days simply flowed over them like a river surging over shallow steps. Effortlessly, he was *still* extending his lead. Rachel continued to praise him at every jump.

Now, as they swung into the last bend of the oval circuit, she decided she must risk a glance to see where the opposition was. To her astonishment, she saw that the nearest challenger (if he could be described thus!) was at least twenty lengths behind her. Yet there were only two hurdles to be overcome before they reached the short straight.

'Come on, Hay Days, we've got to keep going,' she

99

said to herself as much as to the horse.

She'd heard of horses, and jockeys, who'd lost concentration just because they'd been out in front on their own for so long. Rachel was determined that wasn't going to happen to them. So far the chestnut had shown no signs whatsoever of running out of steam. He was galloping with all the relentless energy he'd displayed at the beginning of the race. For the first time since she'd set off from the paddock she had an inkling that not only could they win   they were going to! Her main concern was to ensure that Hay Days didn't make a mistake at either of the remaining obstacles.

The horse, though, must have known what was in her mind. For he treated both flights of hurdles with respect. There was no semblance of an error in his jumping and his momentum wasn't checked. Still there were no sounds of pursuit but Rachel wasn't going to look round again. Her only aim now was to keep the horse going. And it was only as the winning-post rushed towards them that, at last, Hay Days' speed slackened a little.

Only Chapel Row managed to stage something of a challenge and his final run took him well clear of the remainder. By then, however, the race as a spectacle was over. Hay Days had triumphed without really being tested or, of course, being shown the whip. In every sense, it was a bloodless victory.

Rachel, as she pulled him up, couldn't believe how easy it had been. It was really only when she saw the stable lad's face, aglow with delight, and received calls of congratulation and even handshakes from other riders, that it sank in that she had actually won the race. Her first ever success as a jockey!

'Fantastic, fantastic!' Billy Allaway was chortling as he rushed out to greet her on the triumphal procession to the winner's enclosure. 'You did everything we could have asked for – and better than we could have asked for! Great, great performance, Rachel.'

There was only a scattering of applause from spectators for hardly anyone could have backed the 25–1 winner. As she heard the price being announced Rachel fleetingly thought of Mr Thornton. He'd be mad with himself if he hadn't put some money on Hay Days!

The greeting as they entered the enclosure was warmer and Rachel happily posed for photographs with her winner. Several more people came up to say, 'Well done!' and one of them was Jake Cooper, apparently none the worse for his tumble from the favourite.

'Even if I hadn't been unseated I'd never have won the way you were going,' he said. 'I'm sure everybody else thought you'd come back to us, run out of juice, but this horse has obviously got ability and stamina. And you'd had the good sense to walk the course last time, hadn't you? So you knew what you were up to. I'm very pleased indeed for you, Rachel.'

There seemed to be so much excitement around her that Rachel had to be reminded by Mr Allaway to go and weigh-in: if she failed to do that the horse would be disqualified! As she left, after giving Hay Days a final grateful pat, she could hear the trainer doing his best to convince reporters that he had no idea the horse could win at all, let alone in that fashion. Later, when she read the sports pages, she was to discover how generous were his tributes to her abilities as a rider.

Eventually, after completing all the necessary routine tasks and then changing back into her working-clothes, she was on her own again with time to savour her blissful experience of winning her first race. Her only regret was that she hadn't been partnering Catch Boy. To her astonishment she suddenly realised that for the first time for as long as she could remember, her favourite horse hadn't held first place in her thoughts during the past hour or so. He was due to run in the third race, the Aspiring Novices Hurdle, and so it was high time she went off to see that he was all right.

Then she hesitated. Perhaps that wasn't such a good idea after all. Nicola would be preparing him for his race and certainly wouldn't want to share her responsibilities with Rachel, whose friendship with Catch Boy she clearly resented at times. Quite possibly, Nicola might also display some jealousy now that Rachel had ridden a winner. So Rachel reluctantly decided to stay away from the racecourse stables for the present and instead watch the next race, a handicap steeplechase in which Bryn McWilliam was riding a horse called Toscanini for another stable. Already the runners were down at the start and so she hurried off to find a vantage point.

When the race started Toscanini soon showed he didn't think much of being asked to jump fences. At the first he slowed down almost to a walk, hesitated, and then seemed to take it almost sideways; he was hardly more efficient at the second but somehow scrambled over it lengths behind the rest of the field. The third obstacle was sited practically in front of the grandstand and Bryn gave his mount a couple of hearty thwacks to encourage him to take it properly.

The outcome was calamitous. Toscanini simply dived into the fence instead of over it and turned a complete somersault as he came down. Bryn was thrown clear but landed crunchingly on his head and one shoulder. As the horse got to its feet and charged off, the jockey remained motionless.

'That's him done for,' remarked a spectator beside Rachel in an unsympathetic tone. 'Never gave the horse a chance of showing what it could do.'

Rachel was sickened by the accident and the sight of the ambulance-men removing Bryn from the centre of the track before the runners returned to that point. So far as she could tell he was unconscious. The race no longer held any interest for her and she pushed her way out of the stand as, with the favourite now moving to the front, excitement among spectators began to mount. She and Bryn would never be friends and, in fact, they'd hardly exchanged a word since that incident in the tack room when she'd slapped his face, but the thought that he might be badly injured disturbed her greatly. Jockeys expected to fall off or be thrown from time to time; but they also believed they would always escape any real damage to themselves.

The race was over, and she'd absently seen the horses return, when suddenly she realised she was famished. 'Naturally!' she told herself. 'I haven't eaten a thing since breakfast!'

She was on the edge of the crowd heading for the cafeteria when Kevin Huzzard spotted her and grabbed her arm.

'Been looking all over for you, Rachel,' he told her breathlessly. 'Thank goodness I've found you. Will you ride Catch Boy in the next? Mr Cayley himself has offered you the ride.'

'What!' She really couldn't believe what she was hearing. It was even more amazing than winning on Hay Days. 'But why me?'

'He says you've now got winning form and that's important to him. You've proved you can succeed. We need another rider because Bryn is concussed and therefore he can't ride for another seven days at least. That's official. So, come on, what do you say, Ray? We've no time to waste.'

'Oh yes, please! And thank you, thank you very much.'

'Good girl. I know you get on with the horse and that's the main thing. Right, let's get going.'

So, within a very few minutes she was back in the makeshift women's changing-room, putting on her breeches and Richard Cayley's gold-and-blue colours. It occurred to her then that those colours weren't so very different from Hay Days' – and *they* had proved lucky for her. In the weighing-room she got one or two curious looks from jockeys who'd never seen her before; and, suddenly, it struck her that this time she would be riding against *professionals*. But, with race-time rapidly approaching, she wasn't going to dwell on that thought. In any case, she was obviously riding with the full approval of another professional racing man, Kevin Huzzard.

In the parade ring Richard Cayley greeted her with a wide smile and a lift of his grey hat and she responded by touching the peak of her cap as a salute. In the most courteous way possible, the owner tried to convince her that she was doing him a favour by accepting the ride. Inevitably, that boosted her ego considerably.

'Just do your best and then we'll have no complaints,' Mr Huzzard told her. 'If you're as calm as you were on your winner then you won't go far wrong.'

When she went over to mount Catch Boy she received a rather grudging half-smile from Nicola in response to her own friendly grin. But the stable-girl could hardly pass any unfavourable comment in the presence of the guv'nor.

Rachel had already heard the tannoyed announcement about the change of rider for Catch Boy and she intercepted a number of curious glances from the public lining the rails as she made her way down to the start. Some people, realising that she'd already had one winner, might well go and have a bet on the bay on the grounds that it seemed to be her lucky day. They'd get good odds because Catch Boy had no known form while both the first and second favourites, Chase Bridge and Kaskaskia, were thought to be among the best young hurdlers in the country. What's more, Chase Bridge was being partnered by the season's leading jockey.

Before lining up for the start of the two-mile race she gave Catch Boy a chance to have a good look at the kind of obstacle he'd be jumping; that was something most jockeys did and it made sense even though all the hurdles were of a regulation pattern. As soon as the tape went up Rachel's tension departed: she was riding her favourite horse and they were going to enjoy themselves. Nobody was expecting them to win but they were going to do their best. Whatever happened, she would at last have ridden against professional jockeys. Because she was riding Catch Boy she would achieve two ambitions in one race. The inner glow of satisfaction was very warming indeed.

A dark bay called Sandbar surged into the lead and there was little jostling for position even as they approached the first, relatively sharp bend. Catch Boy had placed himself in the middle of the main bunch of runners and was lobbing along happily. To

Rachel's satisfaction he had flipped over the first obstacle without apparent effort. The pace was undemanding and already she was enjoying herself.

She wanted Catch Boy to be relaxed, and he was. Her only worry concerned the two hurdles close together down the back straight. It was there, last time, that Bryn had hit the horse and Catch Boy struck the top of the hurdle. Then, because of a collision with another horse, Bryn fell off. Horses sometimes remembered bad moments and exactly where trouble had happened. But, as they now approached that point, Catch Boy, if he had any worries, wasn't communicating them to her.

A horse closed right in on them from the outside as they prepared themselves for the first jump and, momentarily, Rachel feared they were going to be barged out of the way. But his jockey straightened him up as they both took off. Catch Boy cleared the hurdle faultlessly but then seemed to flinch as someone alongside them slapped hard at his mount.

'It's all right, Boy, it's all right,' Rachel assured him, hoping that it would be as they went for the second jump.

Now the air seemed to be full of voices and the clatter of hooves as they met the swinging hurdle, two sections of which had already been knocked out of the ground by the leaders, Sandbar and Kaskaskia. Within the space of a few strides the pace hotted up dramatically. A horse directly ahead of Catch Boy swerved against the whip as his jockey gave him a

sharp reminder to keep going. Rachel knew she was in a very different kind of race from the first one of the afternoon.

With the final sweeping bend coming up rapidly and Sandbar falling back, beaten, changes were taking place all around her. Catch Boy was still going easily but now she wanted him to quicken. He had to make progress past fading horses and be in the right position to make his effort in the straight. Then, just as she was trying to manoeuvre towards the running rail a horse loomed up in the gap on her left. A quick glance told her it was Chase Bridge the favourite, plainly determined to take the shortest route home.

Together they took the third last hurdle in their stride. Just ahead of them Kaskaskia and Decanter, a very pale grey, were racing together and leading the field. Catch Boy, though, gave her the feeling that he still had plenty of power in the tank: he was running as sweetly as she could wish. Her hopes that she could feature in the finish were rising. Her only worry was about when to unleash their run. Correct timing was vital.

Over the second last Kaskaskia and Decanter were still matching strides, as were Catch Boy and Chase Bridge. Rachel risked a look across at her rival but the leading jockey didn't return it. She thought he appeared tense and worried. That elated her. Perhaps she had the beating of the favourite after all!

Then, as they approached the final obstacle, a gap opened up between the leaders. Was this the moment for her to strike? Should she go for it and hope for the best?

Before she even had time to ask Catch Boy to quicken, Chase Bridge swept past them as if he'd found another gear. Within seconds his hindquarters were disappearing through the gap between the leaders – a gap that closed swiftly just as Catch Boy,

responding to Rachel's urgings, made his move. Now she had to snatch him up again to avoid a collision with Kaskaskia who, finding the pressure too great for him, was stopping.

Her chance had gone. She realised that immediately. The jockey on Chase Bridge had also been deciding when to pounce – and his professional reaction had been faster than Rachel's. He'd seen his opportunity and seized it without a split-second's delay. The favourite had forged ahead and there was no hope of anyone catching him on that short run-in to the winning-post.

Decanter ran on gamely to be second and Catch Boy, ridden out with hands and heels only, finished third, comfortably ahead of the one-paced Kaskaskia.

'Great, that was great, Boy!' she told him, slapping his neck as they pulled up.

So it was, as Kevin Huzzard and Richard Cayley told her when she rode into the unsaddling enclosure. After all, as they pointed out, the horse had never before finished in the first three of any race.

'You really couldn't have done any better, Rachel, you rode him splendidly,' the trainer wanted to assure her. 'You had no chance with the winner, you know.'

'Oh, yes I could,' she replied before going to weigh-in. 'If I'd timed things better we could have been second. But next time – next time, we're going to win. If – if you give me another chance to ride him.'

'No doubt about that, Rachel,' the owner said with a smile. 'On today's form alone, you've earned it.'

*These and other Magnet Books are available at your
bookshop or newsagent. In case of difficulties, orders may
be sent to:*

Magnet Books
Cash Sales Department
PO Box 11
Falmouth Cornwall TR10 9EN
England

Please send cheque or postal order, no currency,
for purchase price quoted and allow the following
for postage and packing:

UK CUSTOMERS

Please allow 55p for the first book, plus 22p for the
second book and 14p for each additional book
ordered, to a maximum charge of £1.75.

BFPO & EIRE

Please allow 55p for the first book,
plus 22p for the second book and 14p for
the next 7 books, thereafter 8p per book.

OVERSEAS CUSTOMERS

Please allow £1.00 for the first book, plus 25p
per copy for each additional book.

While every effort is made to keep prices low,
it is sometimes necessary to increase prices at
short notice. Magnet Books reserves the right
to show new retail prices on covers which may differ
from those previously advertised in the text
or elsewhere.